# Gilmore girls

## The Other Side of Summer

ADAPTED BY HELEN PAI
FROM THE TELEVISION SERIES CREATED BY
AMY SHERMAN-PALLADINO,
FROM THE TELEPLAY "NICK & NORA/SID & NANCY"
WRITTEN BY AMY SHERMAN-PALLADINO,
THE TELEPLAY "PRESENTING LORELAI GILMORE . . ."
WRITTEN BY SHEILA R. LAWRENCE,
THE TELEPLAY "LIKE MOTHER, LIKE DAUGHTER"
WRITTEN BY JOAN BINDER WEISS,
THE TELEPLAY "THE INS AND OUTS OF INNS"
WRITTEN BY DANIEL PALLADINO,
AND THE TELEPLAY "RUN AWAY, LITTLE BOY"
WRITTEN BY JOHN STEPHENS

HarperEntertainment
*An Imprint of HarperCollinsPublishers*

HARPERENTERTAINMENT
*An Imprint of* HarperCollins*Publishers*
10 E. 53rd Street
New York, New York 10022-5299

ISBN: 0-06-050916-3

First HarperEntertainment paperback printing: November 2002

Printed in the United States of America

Visit HarperEntertainment on the World Wide Web at
www.harpercollins.com

10 9 8 7 6 5 4 3 2 1

# Gilmore girls

## 1

Have you ever noticed that there's a disturbingly large number of songs written about school ending and summer vacation, but very few about the fall and returning to your studies? Trust me, I know, I've done research with both of my best friends—Lane Kim, who is about all things music, and my mom, Lorelai Gilmore, who is just about all things. We finally found a song by the White Stripes, a band out of Detroit, Michigan, comprised of Jack and Meg White. "We're Going to Be Friends" is simple, almost Beatles-esque in tone, and is about the joys of childhood and the excitement one has when they first start school.

Apparently there's some controversy as to whether Jack and Meg are siblings or former husband and wife, but to me the bigger question is how did a band out of Detroit, automobile capital of the world, and a city better known for giving us Alice Cooper, Iggy Pop, and Eminem, breed a band that could write such an innocent and endearing song?

Now, don't get me wrong. I like summers. I think

summers are great. I just really happen to love school and I feel that excitement the White Stripes sing about whenever I think about school. So, it is with great anticipation that I sit at Luke's Diner having breakfast with my mom on the first day of the fall semester. There is no better place to start off the day than Luke's. He has, hands down, the best coffee in the world, though I wouldn't know that for sure as I haven't really traveled much outside my hometown of Stars Hollow, Connecticut. But that will change when I become the next Christiane Amanpour and travel around the world, reporting on what's going on, and, of course, trying out the coffee everywhere I go so I can stand behind my aforementioned statement.

Of course, in order to get there, I have to finish high school and get into Harvard, the university of my dreams, and that requires actually getting to the place of education. So I quickly finished my breakfast and sat watching Mom eat hers. I stared at her anxiously.

"How are the eggs?" I finally asked, hoping to speed her up.

"Good," Mom answered.

"I'm glad," I said.

Mom kept eating and I continued to stare, tapping my fingers impatiently.

"They're still good," Mom said, looking up at me.

"I'm still glad."

"Look, freak, we will not be late."

"It's the first day of school, I want to get there early."

"We will get there early. I promise."

"I have different classes this year. My routes aren't the same. I haven't found the quickest path around. And my locker, they moved it so I don't even know if it will work properly and then I'll have to get a new one and God knows how long that will take or where it'll be and that could send the whole day into chaos." Mom smiled at me. "I'm just excited," I completed, returning the smile.

Lane came bursting through the door. "Oh, thank God you haven't left yet," she said as she rushed to our table and sat down.

"Nope . . . what's up?" I asked.

"Well, I found the greatest record store in the world, it's ten minutes from your school, and I'm wondering how much you love me," Lane said, putting down her backpack.

What kind of crazy question was that? Next to my mom, she's been my best friend forever. I would do anything for her.

"Address," I said as I leaned over to get a piece of paper and pen out of my bag.

"Record Breaker, Incorporated. 2453 Berlin Turnpike."

I wrote it down. "Got it. Place your order now."

"Yes," Lane said, excited. She pulled out her well-worn copy of *The MOJO Collection* and flipped it open. *The MOJO Collection*, a monstrous book that presents a guide to the history of the pop album, is put out by the fine people at *MOJO*, the U.K.'s leading rock magazine. The magazine commissioned leading music journalists to select what they considered the most important albums ever recorded and reassess their significance to popular music. Lane, following their lead, has since reassessed her CD collection, deemed it insufficient and was trying to correct it.

"Charles Mingus, *The Black Saint and the Sinner Lady*," Lane said, reading from the book.

"Right," I said, jotting it down.

"The Sonics, *Here Are the Sonics*."

"Burn me a copy. Next."

"MC5, *Kick Out the Jams*, Fairport Convention, *Liege and Lief*, Bee Gees, *Odessa* . . ."

"Bee Gees. Really," I said, surprised.

She shut the book and placed her hand reverentially on it. "Well, *MOJO* says . . ."

"So it must be true."

"Okay, that's it. Now, if I can just find a copy of Whistler, Chaucer, Detroit and Greenhill, I will finally be done with the sixties," Lane said, handing me some money.

"I'll get there today. Tomorrow at the latest," I promised.

"I love it when you go back to school," she said with a huge smile.

"Me too," I said, returning the smile. Mom got up and started for the counter. "Hey!" I yelled at her.

"I am getting doughnuts for later," she replied. "As soon as I do I'll drive you to school and the nice men in white coats will pick you up."

Taylor Doose, owner of Doose's Market and self-appointed town leader, passed by with his Boy Scout troop and Mom stood to the side, waiting impatiently while they argued about what they were ordering. Finally, she interrupted. "Hey, doughnuts, please."

"We were here first," one of the kids said.

"On the planet?" Mom replied.

"Huh?" was the confused kid's response.

"You lose," Mom said and then turned to Luke. "Chocolate, cinnamon, and sprinkles."

Before Luke could get anyone's food, the phone rang and everyone groaned.

"Come on!" Mom said.

"All of you pipe down!" Luke ordered.

He answered the phone and we all watched him impatiently. Mom finally went around behind the counter, grabbed a bag, and started putting some doughnuts into it. I got up, one step closer to getting to school.

"This is unbelievable!" Luke yelled into the phone. Everyone turned and stared at him. "You won't ever change, will you? Okay, fine! Do what you want! Make the arrangements. Now, I'm working. We'll finish this later!" and he slammed the phone down.

"Is everything okay?" Mom asked.

"Do you have a sister?" Luke wanted to know.

"Uh . . . no," Mom replied.

"I do," one of the kids piped up.

"You have my sympathies," Luke said as he headed upstairs to his office/apartment.

Mom watched him go until I reminded her time was a-tickin'. She grabbed her bag of doughnuts and finally I was on my way to school.

Mom dropped me off at the imposing gates of Chilton Prep School, and I headed inside. The halls were filled with uniformed kids looking for their lockers and classrooms. A "Welcome Back to Chilton" banner was hanging on the wall. I was a few minutes early, so I found my locker, dropped some books in there, then headed to my first class. As I approached the classroom door, Paris Geller and her best friends Madeline Lynn and Louise Grant came up from the opposite direction. Paris stared icily at me for a moment before continuing on into the room. "Okay. Round two." I sighed.

Paris Geller despises me for so many reasons, mostly just because I exist. She marched up to me on my first day at Chilton last year and asked if I was going out for *The Franklin*, the school paper. Then she went on to tell me she was going to be the editor, that she was currently the top of our class, and that she intended to be valedictorian when she graduated. And things went downhill from there. It was extremely tiring being

hated by Paris, and, true to her word, she was editor of
*The Franklin* this year, and I was on staff. I walked into
the classroom and went straight to Paris. "Five seconds?" I asked.

"Four."

"Fine."

"Now it's three."

"Paris, it does not have to be like this."

"No?"

"You and I are going to have to spend a lot of time in
class together and on *The Franklin*."

"I know."

"We're going to have to sit in the same room, share
the same oxygen, occasionally make eye contact . . ."

"I can avoid that," she replied.

"Look, I'm not saying that we should be friends, I
don't want to be friends. I'm just saying that maybe we
should look at this like life."

"Life?" Paris asked.

"Yes. In life there will be people you don't like but
that you have to coexist with."

"I am well aware of that."

"So, I'm just suggesting that we coexist." I thought it
was a reasonable request, but Paris didn't agree.

"You're just scared that I'm going to make your life
on *The Franklin* a living hell. Especially since I'm the editor and you're . . . oh, what's the word, not," Paris said.

"If you want to spend the precious energy that you
would normally spend on the paper obsessing on ways
to make me miserable, then that's your choice. I'm just
suggesting an alternate plan," I stated.

Paris considered this for a moment.

"The paper could be really great this year," I continued.

"I know," Paris said, a little defensively.

"Can't we just agree on that and let the other stuff go away?" I said.

Louise and Madeline came over.

"Everything okay?" Louise asked.

"Yeah, Riff. Everything's fine," I responded.

"We were just talking," Paris said.

"Talking? You two?" Madeline asked.

"About *The Franklin*," Paris continued.

"Oh." Madeline thought a moment. "Nope, still seems weird."

"Hey, look, we're all on the paper together, there's going to be a lot of long afternoons, and weekends . . ." Paris said.

"Weekends?" Louise interrupted.

"We need to coexist," Paris said as she looked at me. "Right?"

"Right," I replied, a little surprised my speech worked.

"I'm sorry," Louise said, "back up to the weekends."

"Okay, so that's what we'll do," Paris said, ignoring Louise. "Now, the first meeting of *The Franklin* is today."

"Yes, it is," I said.

"Four o'clock," Paris continued.

"Sounds good," I said.

Paris and I looked at each other a moment. It appeared a truce had been reached. We took our seats and settled in for class.

"Weekends were never mentioned. I need my weekends. All of this gets done on weekends!" Louise continued complaining, gesturing to her hair, face, and body.

As class started, I glanced at Paris and smiled, pleased.

Around ten till four, I headed over to *The Franklin*'s newsroom. Since I was a little early, I sat on the bench outside the newsroom and pulled *Selected Letters of Dawn Powell* out of my backpack. Powell was a prolific novelist best known for her stinging wit. A little stinging wit never hurt a girl, I say, so I settled in to read while I waited for the other news staffers to arrive. After a few minutes, I realized I was hearing voices from inside the room, so I went in to discover the entire news team assembled and the meeting in progress. Paris was at the head of the long conference table addressing the group, which included Mrs. O'Malley, the paper's adviser.

"The op-ed page is sad. It's worse than sad. It's unopinionated. Pick a side, people," Paris was saying as I entered. "Oh, Rory," she said, stopping so everyone could see me walk in.

"Hey," I said, confused.

"Nice of you to join us, Ms. Gilmore," Mrs. O'Malley said.

"I . . . I thought we were starting at four," I stammered.

"No. We start at three-fifteen sharp," Mrs. O'Malley replied.

I tried to explain, but Paris interrupted. "Look, we're wasting time here."

I glared at Paris. Apparently the truce was off. Mrs. O'Malley asked me to take a seat, and Paris continued the meeting.

"Okay, so we were just finishing up handing out the first assignments. Now, Rory, unfortunately since you got here so late most everything of interest has been given out."

"Why, I'm shocked," I said.

"Wait, wait, just let me check my list here. There might be something left for you."

I shook my head in frustration at Paris's innocent act.

"Okay, well, here," she continued. "They're paving the new parking lot."

"And?"

"And, you can cover it."

"Cover what?"

"The paving process."

"You're serious?"

"Absolutely. I'm sure there's an angle there somewhere. Is it environmentally safe? What are the financial ramifications? Should brick have been considered, especially taking into account the architecture of the building . . . ?"

"Yeah, yeah, I get the idea," I told her.

"But hey," Paris went on, looking directly at me, "if you think this is below you, you can always wait until the next issue. You can just use this time to get a nice manicure."

"That's okay," I told her.

"Maybe get a massage."

"I'll do it."

"Aromatherapy. Smell like a peach for a few days."

"I said I'll do it, okay? I'll cover the paving." I gave Paris my best false smile.

"Okay. Good. Well, then I guess that's it."

Everyone got up from the table and dispersed. Paris went over to one of the computer stations and I followed her.

"Problem, Ms. Gilmore?" Paris said, not looking up from the screen.

"Nope. No problem at all. I love this assignment."

"I'm glad."

"I am going to write the greatest piece about pavement you've ever read."

"I hope so."

"And next week when you give me the scoop on the new copper plumbing installation, I'm going to be just as thrilled."

"I like a team player."

"And no matter how many crappy, stupid, useless assignments you throw at me, I'm not going to quit and I'm not going to back down. So you can go home tonight and think about the fact that no matter what you do and no matter how evil you are, at the end of the year on my high school transcript it's going to say that I worked on *The Franklin*. So, if you'll excuse me I have some reading to do on the origins of concrete." I turned and walked away from her.

"A thousand words on my desk on Tuesday!" she called out after me.

And things got worse. As I headed down the hallway, I ran right into Max Medina, my English teacher and my mom's super-recent ex-fiancé. This was the first time we'd seen each other since she called off the wedding and neither of us knew what to do or how to react. So we did what came naturally. Max tried to talk to me, and I bolted in the other direction before he could get anything out.

On the bus ride home, the shock of seeing Max had worn off and I started thinking about how Paris tricked me into showing up late to the first *Franklin* meeting of the year. By the time I met Mom at Luke's, I was really pissed off.

"Oh my God, I hate her!" I said as I entered the diner.

"Oh, me too!" my Mom agreed.

"You have no idea who I'm talking about."

"Solidarity, sister.

I sat down next to Mom and took a sip of her coffee, then explained. "Paris . . ."

"Ugh, well, that I should've guessed," Mom said.

"She thinks she can torture me off the paper and she can't," I continued.

"No, she can't," Mom supported.

"I have never met anyone like her before. Her insistence on holding on to this stupid grudge that is based on nothing and will never ever end shows an amount of commitment that I would have never thought possible. I'm beginning to admire her."

"First day sucked?" Mom asked.

"Just the paper stuff sucked. The rest of the stuff was good."

"Good, I'm glad to hear it." She paused for a second before proceeding. "Did you . . . happen to run into Max?"

It was my turn to stop a moment. "Actually, no."

"Really?" Mom seemed a little surprised.

"Yeah. Our paths just didn't cross," I said carefully.

"Isn't he your lit teacher?" Mom asked.

"Yeah, but I do have really tall people sitting in front of me," I said.

"Rory . . ."

"I saw him in the hall and I walked the other way and—"

"Why?"

"I don't know. I thought that's what you'd want me to do."

"Just because Max isn't a part of my life anymore doesn't mean he can't be part of yours. He has to be part of yours. You have to see him and talk to him and that's okay. That's good. I know everything seems screwed up right now but I don't want you to avoid him. Especially not on my account. Okay?"

"All right."

"I'm sorry that I put you in this position," Mom said gently.

"That's okay. It's going on the list," I replied.

"My God, that list's getting long," Mom said with a smile.

"You have no idea." I smiled back. "Home?"

"Right behind you."

We got up to head out when Mom asked one of her world famous random questions. "Hey, how are we on paper plates?"

"I don't know. Let me look at the extremely detailed log I'm keeping on our monthly paper plate supply," I replied. What else can one say to that sort of question?

"Okay, if you're taking my sarcasm I want my blue flip-flops back," Mom said.

"I think we're low," I answered as we headed out the door. "Why?"

"We are having a little gathering tomorrow night," Mom explained as we headed home.

"What kind of gathering?" I wanted to know.

"Well, Luke's nephew is here and I thought we could try and help him feel a little more at home," Mom explained.

I was kind of surprised. I didn't know Luke had a nephew. She went on to tell me his nephew, Jess, was moving to Stars Hollow.

"Did you meet him?" I asked.

"Sort of."

"What's he like?"

"Well, he's not gonna be subbing for that new dodo on the *Regis* show anytime soon, let's put it like that."

We continued down the street toward Doose's Market, passing the library, which reminded me that though I'd love to take part in whatever pre–Welcome to Stars Hollow dinner preparations were necessary, they would all have to be restricted to research on pavement. Mom agreed, on the condition that that research in-

cluded Pavement the band. We finally came to the conclusion that I would only listen to the band Pavement
while doing my research on pavement. I ran off to the
library to start my article, and Mom continued home.

∽

The next afternoon, I returned to *The Franklin* newsroom. I had turned my article in earlier and I was sitting
in the room, alone, reading, when Paris entered.

"Oh. Hello," she said, a little startled to see me.

"Hi," I replied.

"You're early."

"Yeah, well, I felt so bad about the mix-up last time I
wanted to make sure it didn't happen again." I smiled
smugly at her. "It won't."

Paris took her place at the end of the table, directly
across from me, as people started filing in.

"Hey. Did you hear that Kimber Slately and Tristin
are a major major item?" Madeline said as she entered
with Louise.

"I thought Kimber and Sean Asher were this year's
John and Jackie," Louise replied.

"Nope. Sean is with Deeds McGuire now. Which
pushed Jeff Trainer into Dottie Lords's arms, leaving
Madison Malins alone for the first weekend since he became captain of the lacrosse team."

Louise was impressed. "You know so much so soon.
You have the gift."

"I know," Madeline replied. "Hey, Paris, what do
you think about me writing a gossip column for *The
Franklin*?"

"Huh," she replied. "I don't know. That's a hard one.
I mean, this is *The Franklin*, a newspaper that's been
around for almost a hundred years. There have been at

least ten former editors of *The Franklin* that have gone on to work at the *New York Times*. Six have gone on to the *Washington Post*. Three are contributing editors at the *New Yorker*. I think one even went on to win the Pulitzer Prize. But never mind them. I could be the first editor in the history of *The Franklin* to introduce a column exclusively devoted to who Biffy's boffing today. Quandary. You know, I'm going to have to get back to you on that one."

Madeline had to think about that for a second. "Okay," she said, still not completely sure what Paris meant.

Mrs. O'Malley came into the room holding a stack of papers and addressed the group. "Oh, good, we're all here. And prompt," she added, looking at me. "Lovely. Well, I have read everyone's article. They were all extremely well done. Snappy, informative, well researched . . . Paris, you should be very proud of the team you have assembled here this year."

"Thank you." Paris smiled, pleased with the compliment.

"I mean, when you've got a reporter who can take an incredibly mundane and seemingly unimportant subject like the repaving of the faculty parking lot and turn it into a bittersweet piece on how everybody and everything eventually becomes obsolete, then you've really got something. Ms. Gilmore, I was touched." Paris shifted uncomfortably in her chair.

"I owe it all to Paris," I said as Paris smiled falsely at me.

Mrs. O'Malley turned to Paris. "I would strongly advise that next time you give Ms. Gilmore something with a little more meat to it."

"Oh. Yeah. Great idea," Paris replied.

Mrs. O'Malley proceeded to get the newsroom

working on the layout and I went over to one of the computer stations and sat down. Paris marched over to me. "Well, congratulations," she said.

"Thank you," I replied, looking up at her.

"You must be very proud of yourself," she continued.

"I'm not hiding when I pass a mirror," I answered.

"I guess it's part of my job as editor to make sure that our best writers are writing our best pieces. So . . . I'm going to give you one of our best pieces."

I looked at her suspiciously. "Uh huh . . ."

"Front page. Lead story. Above the fold."

"Get to the catch, Paris."

"No catch."

"No catch," I repeated skeptically.

"I'd like to start our year off with a profile on the teacher voted most popular from the year before. You know, an in-depth, no-holds-barred interview. Everybody wants it. You have it," Paris said sincerely.

"You're kidding," I said, still a little wary.

"Nope."

She really didn't seem to be kidding. "Well, thanks," I said as I turned back to the computer.

"You're welcome. So, go ahead and set up that interview with Mr. Medina as soon as possible."

"What?"

"I know it's short notice but I'd love it to lead off our first edition."

"Mr. Medina?"

"He was the winner by a landslide."

"But . . ."

"I'm sorry, is there a problem?"

I didn't know how to answer that so I didn't reply.

Paris thrilled in my hesitation. "I mean, is there some reason why you wouldn't want to interview him? After all, you of all people should be able to get the most in-depth story out of him, especially since he and your mother are involved."

I continued my silence.

"They are still involved, aren't they?" Paris continued with mock concern.

"Let's keep my mother's personal life out of this, okay?"

"Oh. That sounds bad," Paris said.

"It's not bad, it's just none of your business," I told her.

"Fine. You want the interview or not?"

I wrestled with it for a moment, then finally answered her. "Yes. I want the interview."

"Good. Get me something more than his favorite color, okay?"

An extremely self-satisfied Paris walked away. How did Paris know something had happened between Max and my mom? She must have seen our run-in yesterday after I left the newsroom. It certainly wouldn't be the first time Paris saw exactly what I didn't want her to see — shortly after I started at Chilton she witnessed my mom and Max making out in his classroom. Yes, not the best judgment on their part, but of all the students at Chilton, Paris is the one to see them? This was an important article, though, and all I needed to do now was to see if there was any way to write it without actually interviewing Max.

## 2

That night was the big dinner. And I mean that literally. My mother's best friend, Sookie St. James, was planning a feast Henry the Eighth would have been proud of. She wanted to make sure Luke's nephew felt welcome and had options ("What if he doesn't do dairy?" she had sensibly asked), so she and her boyfriend, Jackson, were in the kitchen preparing the pot roast, chicken wings, mashed potatoes, four different kinds of salad, and I believe I just heard the words "grilled cheese."

While they were cooking, I started to compile my questions for the interview with Max. I finally arrived at the conclusion that a good journalist is supposed to be objective, thus putting her personal feelings aside, so I set up a meeting with Max for the next afternoon. Mom poked her head in and asked if I was going to join the festivities.

"In a sec," I replied, focusing on the computer screen in front of me.

"You sound crabby," Mom said.

"I'm concentrating."

"Okay, don't concentrate too hard. The boys like 'em dumb. Right, Jackson?"

"If you can navigate yourself around a tree, keep on walking," Jackson called back from the kitchen.

There was a knock at the door and Mom went off to answer it. A few minutes later, Luke and his nephew Jess came into the kitchen, and Mom introduced them to Sookie and Jackson. I was still sitting at my desk so I turned around to say a quick hello, then started to put my stuff away so I could join them. Jess looked like he was around my age and had dark eyes and dark hair. He wandered into my room.

"I'm Rory."

"Yeah, I figured."

"Nice to meet you."

Jess started walking over to my desk but stopped when he noticed all the books lining the shelves. "Wow, aren't we hooked on phonics."

"Oh, I read a lot," I responded. "Do you read?"

"Not much." He opened up my copy of Allen Ginsberg's *Howl*.

"I could loan you that if you want. It's great."

Jess closed the book and tossed it down. "No, thanks."

"Well, if you change your mind . . ."

He continued over to me as Mom walked in holding two huge bowls of food and announced that they were moving the feast into the living room.

"Be right there," I said as Sookie, Jackson, and Luke also walked past carrying bowls and plates of food. Jess pushed aside the lace curtain covering the window. "So, do these open?"

"Oh yeah, you just have to unlatch them and then push," I said.

"Great," he said as he unlatched the window. "Shall we?"

"Shall we what?"

"Bail."

"No," I said, laughing.

"Why?"

"Because it's Tuesday night in Stars Hollow. There's nowhere to bail to. The twenty-four-hour mini-mart closed twenty minutes ago."

"So, we'll walk around, or sit on a bench and stare at our shoes."

"Look, Sookie just made a ton of really great food, and I'm starving, and though it may not seem like it right at this moment, it's gonna be fun. Trust me," I said with a smile.

"I don't even know you."

"Well, don't I look trustworthy?"

"Maybe."

"Okay, good, let's eat."

I walked out of my room and to the fridge. Jess slowly followed. "You want a soda?" I asked.

"Oh, I'll get it," he replied.

"Okay." And I went off to the living room to join the others. A large table had been set up in the middle of the room and Sookie was arranging the platters of food. I sat down next to my mom.

"Hey, Rory, where's Jess?" Luke asked.

"He's getting a soda," I replied.

Mom handed Luke a plate piled sky-high with food. "Here."

"I'm sorry, you must've mistaken me for you," Luke said.

"Oh, too much?" Mom took the plate back and added another dollop of mashed potatoes.

"Ooh, I forgot the garlic bread," Sookie said.

"I'll get it," Mom said as she handed Luke his even bigger plate back and walked out to the kitchen.

Mom was gone for a while, and Jess still hadn't shown up at the table so Luke got up to check on them. A short while later, Mom returned to the table with the garlic bread, looking really pissed off. She told us Luke and Jess were gone and they wouldn't be joining us for dinner. And then there were four—with enough food to feed a small country.

∽

The next morning proved to be tricky. Mom was vague about the fight the night before, but it was a big enough deal that she refused to go in to Luke's. So we stood just outside the diner door, and the delicious coffee waited patiently inside.

"You're being completely childish," I said to her.

"Am not," she replied childishly.

"So what, we're never gonna go into Luke's again, we're just going to starve."

"Rory, this was a bad one, okay? This was not Nick and Nora. This was Sid and Nancy and I'm not going in."

"But the coffee is in there. And it's Danish Day. Are you seriously telling me that you're gonna let a stupid fight get in the way of Danish Day?" I said, trying to reason with her.

"No, I'm not."

"Good," I said, relieved.

"So go in there, order two coffees and two Danishes to go," Mom said.

"You're kidding, right?"

"Don't forget the napkins."

"Mom, he's gonna know what's going on. He's not stupid."

"Hey, he cannot prove that you aren't ordering all this for yourself, can he? No. So, go on. Scoot, scoot. Mommy's right here."

I sighed and headed into the diner. Luke was behind the counter so I went straight up to him. "Hey, Luke."

"Rory," he greeted. He seemed friendly enough.

"Um, I'll have two coffees and two cherry Danishes to go, please," I said.

"Two coffees and two cherry Danishes." He looked at me suspiciously.

"Oh, and some napkins," I added.

"One of these is for her, isn't it?"

"Who? Oh. No, no, no. They're all for me. I am super hungry today. I was debating ordering three, but I'll tell you how I feel after two."

"I'll tell you what, I'll give you one Danish and one cup of coffee, you can sit over there and eat and when you finish them, right over there where I can see you, then I'll bring you the second one."

"You're really just going to stand there and watch me eat a Danish?"

"Cable's out and I'm starved for entertainment."

"Okay, this is insane. So you guys had a fight? Big deal. You know you're going to make up anyway, and what better day to make up than Danish Day. The happiest of all days. The day that we all say, 'Hey, let's forgive and forget' over a nice Danish and a cup of coffee."

"One Danish, one cup of coffee. Take it or leave it."

I sighed. "I'll take it."

Luke went to get the Danish and coffee.

"I still think you're being silly," I told him.

"Thank you for sharing, come back soon." Luke handed me the coffee and a bag with the Danish inside. I grabbed the stuff and headed back outside to Mom.

"Well?" she asked impatiently.

"He would only sell me one."

"Didn't you say they were both for you?"

"Yes. I did. And he knew that I was lying."

"Did you do the blinky thing? You always do the blinky thing when you're lying."

"I didn't have to do the blinky thing, he knows you well enough to know that you're not gonna go a whole day with no coffee and especially no Danish. Why don't you go in there now and just make up?"

"Why don't you . . . give me half your Danish and coffee?"

"I'll give you the Danish," I said, handing her the bag, "but I'm keeping the coffee."

"What is a Danish without coffee?" she asked.

"The eternal question springs up again."

"There's no point in even eating a Danish without coffee."

"I'm going to school."

"Sad Danish. Lonely Danish. Step-Danish."

"I'll see you tonight." And I walked away from my mom and the Danish and went to the bus stop to go to school. I did want my mom to have her coffee and Danish, but I had bigger things to deal with today—today was the interview with Max.

∽

At the appointed time, I headed to Max's classroom. I hesitated for a moment outside the door, briefly considering walking away, but I finally turned the knob and walked in. Max looked equally uncomfortable when I entered, and he jumped up to greet me. "Rory. Hi."

"Am I too early?" I asked, " 'Cause I can—"

"No. No," Max interrupted.

" —come back some other time," I completed.

"This is fine."

"Tomorrow maybe."

"*Now* is good."

I stood there awkwardly. "This is weird."

"Yeah, it is," Max said.

"I don't really know how to act."

"Not completely sure of that myself."

We both continued standing there, not sure what to do next.

"We could sit." Max suggested.

"Sit. Sure. That's good," I said as I finally moved away from the door and into the classroom. "Barbara Walters sits. Or walks sometimes if the person she's talking to has a horse or a ranch or a big backyard sometimes, but usually she just . . . sits."

Max sat back down behind his desk and I pulled a chair over and sat across from him. "Okay, so I guess we should start."

"Good idea," Max said.

I opened up my backpack, took out a pad of paper and a pen, and also a small recorder. "Do you mind if I tape this?"

"Oh. No. Not at all," Max replied.

I set the tape recorder on the desk between us and turned it on. "So, I guess I'll just dive right in. Full name?"

"Max Arturo Medina."

That made me smile. "You're kidding."

"No, I am not."

"Where did that come from?"

"My father's butcher was named Arturo."

"Really?"

"When my mother was pregnant with me she went through a phase where all she would eat was lamb chops. So Arturo would cut her the extra large lamb chops and only charge her for the regular-sized lamb chops, which, in my family, made you eligible for sainthood."

"Hence the Arturo."

"That's right."

"Well, I assume that you are aware that you were overwhelmingly voted the students' favorite teacher last year."

"I teach an exceptional bunch of young people. I'm glad they seem to like me as much as I like them," he replied.

"Have you ever thought of doing something other than teaching?"

"Well, my father wanted me to be a doctor, and my mother wanted me to be president, and I wanted to be . . . a clown."

"What?"

"When I was a kid I went to the circus and I saw this man who was dressed in this crazy outfit and he could juggle and he rode on an elephant and people *loved* him and I thought, Well, that's it. That's for me."

"How long did that last?"

"Junior high. And then slowly I figured out that I wanted to teach. Plus, when you told people that you wanted to be a clown they tended to get very frightened."

"Mom took me to the circus once when I was really little, and this clown knocked into me and I dropped my cotton candy and we didn't have a lot of money back then so she couldn't buy me another one and I started crying. So she literally chased the clown onstage, ripped off his wig, and said she wouldn't give it back to him until he bought me another cotton candy."

"Which I bet he did."

"It was twice as big as the first one and I threw up all the way home."

"Yeah . . . that sounds like your mom," Max said affectionately, reminiscing. I shifted the interview back on track.

"Do you ever regret the fact that you didn't become a clown?" I asked.

"I don't really believe in regrets. All my experiences, even the ones that didn't turn out the way I had wanted them to, I firmly believe they were all worth it."

I looked up at Max, then reached over and turned the tape recorder off. After a moment, I softly said, "I just want you to know, I really wanted you to be my stepfather."

"I just want you to know," Max replied quietly and equally sincere, "I really wanted to be your stepfather."

We looked at each other for a moment and smiled, then I reached over and turned the tape recorder back on to continue the interview.

When I got home, I set myself up in the kitchen and started to work on my Max article. Mom came home a little while later, still crabby about the lack of decent coffee in Stars Hollow and its surrounding counties. Guess that means she still hasn't made up with Luke. As she complained and poured some grounds into the coffee filter, I got up and went to my room.

"Where you going?" she asked. "I'm not through complaining."

"I just have to get some more notes," I told her.

"What's this?" Mom called out to me.

"What?"

"This. This thing you were working on," she said, picking up the pad of paper I had been writing on.

I came back out to the kitchen. "Oh. That's my interview with Max," I told her.

"What interview with Max?" Mom asked.

"The paper wanted to do a piece on the students' favorite teacher from the previous year and Paris assigned it to me once she caught wind of the fact that he and you had—"

"Wow. Nice kid, that Paris," Mom said as she scanned the article.

"Yeah. It wasn't that bad, though."

"No?"

"No. It was actually good. Gave us a chance to talk about some things," I told her.

"Well, good." Mom smiled a little and kept reading.

"Yeah. It was good. Well, I'm gonna buy a folder for it before the store closes," I said as I went back to my room to get some money.

"Okay," Mom said, distracted by what she was reading. "This is some good writing here, missy," she said after a moment.

"Yeah?" I said, heading for the front door.

"Really good."

"It's not quite up to the repaving piece but I'll get it there."

"Boy, he sounds like one hell of a guy, doesn't he," Mom said, a little wistfully.

"Yeah, he does." I smiled and left her with the article.

∽

I bought my folder and started walking home when someone called out. I turned around and saw Jess.

"Hey, yourself," I said.

"What are you doing out here?" Jess asked, walking with me.

"I needed something for school," I replied. "What about you?"

"Oh yeah. Same thing."

"Uh huh. So, that was quite a disappearing act you pulled the other night."

"Potlucks and Tupperware parties aren't really my thing."

"Too cool for school, huh?"

"Yes. That is me."

We walked along in silence for a moment. Jess started fiddling with something in his hands.

"What're you doing?" I asked, stopping.

"Oh, this?" he asked, holding up a coin. "Nothing." He closed his hand around it, opened it back up and the coin was gone. "Just another little disappearing act."

"Little tip?" I said.

"Yeah?"

"If you ever want to speak to me again, don't pull that out of my ear."

"So I assume the nose is off limits, too."

"Any place you wouldn't naturally find a coin, let's leave it at that."

Jess nodded and we started walking again. "So, what are you doing now?" he asked.

"I have some homework to finish," I replied.

"Okay. Then I'll leave you with this last little trick." Jess pulled a copy of *Howl* out of his back pocket. I was surprised.

"You bought a copy? I said I'd loan you mine," I reminded him.

"It is yours," he stated.

I stopped walking. "You stole my book."

"Nope. Borrowed it."

"Okay, see, that's not called a trick, that's called a felony."

"I wanted to put some notes in the margins for you."

"What?" I grabbed the book and flipped through it. "You've read this before," I realized.

"About forty times."

"I thought you said you didn't read much."

"Oh well, what's much?"

Jess smiled and started to walk back toward the diner. "Good night, Rory."

"Good night, Dodger," I replied, still reading the notes he had written in my book.

Jess stopped. "Dodger?"

It was my turn to smile and head off. "Figure it out," I told him.

Jess stood in the street a moment, then called out "*Oliver Twist!*" I nodded and continued home.

When I got there, Mom had two elaborate ice cream sundaes sitting on the kitchen table—a celebration, she said, honoring the return of Danish Day. And as we sat down to consume the tasty treats, Mom finally told me about the fight. At his Welcome to Stars Hollow dinner, Jess snuck a beer out to the back porch. When Mom caught him and didn't bust him, he responded with some inappropriate speculations about her relationship with Luke and then he took off. When Luke came out to find them, Mom told him what had happened and said that he wasn't prepared to handle a kid like Jess. Well, that pissed Luke off, and he told Mom to mind her own business, and he too stormed out. But tonight, just after I left, Luke returned and told my mom she was right after all. He had gotten so frustrated with Jess he didn't know what to do, so he shoved him into the lake and that's when he realized he was in over his head. After Mom found out Jess could swim, she went on to reassure Luke that he would do fine and that Jess was just a seventeen-year-old kid who needed some guidance. Before he left, he reminded Mom to come in the next day for her Danish. "Tomorrow isn't Danish Day," Mom said. "Just be there," Luke replied.

So Sid and Nancy simmered back down to Nick and Nora and the next morning we happily were back at Luke's for coffee and Danish.

# ❧3

Let me take a moment to introduce you to my grandparents, Richard and Emily Gilmore. We have dinner with them every Friday, though this tradition is fairly new. My grandfather went to Yale and is an extremely successful businessman, working as executive vice president at Gehrman-Driscoll Insurance Corporation, one of the largest insurance companies in the country. He oversees the international division, which has taken him to places all over the world, and he shares my love of fine literature. My grandmother is the perfect society wife and is extremely involved in many social and charitable functions. She is also an extremely demanding boss and has a tendency to go through her help. We rarely see the same maid two weeks in a row.

Mom's relationship with them has been rather strained since she got pregnant with me when she was sixteen and opted not to marry my father, Christopher Haden, whose parents are of similar ilk. Instead, she moved out of my grandparents' house shortly after I was born and came to Stars Hollow, where she is now

the manager of the highly regarded Independence Inn.
When I first got accepted to Chilton, Mom had to go to
my grandparents to ask them to loan her the money for
my tuition. They agreed, but only on the condition of
the weekly dinners. It was an extremely hard decision
for my mom, as she spent so many years trying to gain
independence from them, but this was Chilton, which
would hopefully lead me to Harvard, so she agreed and
accepted their terms. I personally enjoy these Friday
night meals, and I think a tiny piece of Mom is starting
to warm up to them as well.

So here we were, Friday night, standing outside my
grandparents' extremely large house in Hartford, waiting for the door to open. Finally, a rather jittery maid
answered the door. "Yes?"

"Hi," Mom said.

"Hello," replied the maid, who was distracted and
kept glancing behind her. Mom and I looked at each
other.

"You're new," Mom said.

"I started yesterday," the maid answered.

"What's your name?" Mom asked.

"Leisal," replied the maid.

"Okay, Leisal, I'm Brigitta, this is Gretel, and I believe Emily and Richard are expecting us," Mom said.

"Oh. I'm sorry. Please, come in."

Liesal kept looking nervously toward the stairwell as
we entered the house. Once inside, we understood why,
as loud arguing voices were heard upstairs.

"Uh, can I, uh, get you a drink?" Leisal offered.

"You know what? That's okay. I can get it. Why
don't you go hide in the kitchen," Mom said.

Leisal was relieved. "Really? Thank you." And she
rushed off.

"What is going on?" I wondered.

"I don't know. I think George and Martha are joining us for dinner," Mom replied as Grandma and Grandpa started coming down the stairs, stopping on the landing. They didn't see us.

"Without telling me!" Grandma was saying.

"I didn't know that my every conversation needed to be reported to you, I stand corrected," Grandpa replied.

"I have been the cochair of the Starlight Foundation for eight years."

"I know this, Emily."

"And the Black-and-White Ball is the main fundraising event of the season."

"It's one year."

"The cochair cannot miss the main fund-raising event."

"Why? Won't the chair be there?"

"Is this a joke to you?"

"Emily, I have too many things to take care of at work. I don't have time for frivolous parties."

"Frivolous parties? Friv . . . ooh!" Grandma responded, fuming.

Furious, Grandma headed back upstairs, Grandpa following. "Where are you going? Come back here."

"Wow. This is bad," I noted.

"I know. I wish we had popcorn," Mom replied.

"Mom . . ."

The voices got louder again.

"Shh. Incoming," Mom said.

Grandma and Grandpa reappeared on the staircase again, Grandma going through a handful of invitations. "The Hartford Zoological Silent Auction. The Mark Twain House Restoration Fund Luncheon. The Harriet Beecher Stowe Literacy Auction."

"I can read those myself you know," Grandpa replied.

"This is the fourth event you have taken upon yourself to turn down on our behalf. And I am on the board of all of those foundations; now how do you think that makes me look?"

"Like your husband is busy and has a great deal of responsibilities."

"Well I have responsibilities too."

"I understand that your social engagements are important—"

"They are not just social engagements."

"Anything at which you serve tea is a social engagement."

"That's it! I'm going to get a tape recorder so you can hear how pompous and condescending you sound," Grandma said, heading back upstairs.

"Emily!" Grandpa called after her.

"No, I wouldn't want you to take my word for it. I might be delirious from all that tea I've been drinking," Grandma said as once again, they disappeared upstairs.

"Maybe we should leave," I said to Mom.

"Are you kidding? We've got dinner theater here."

"But Grandma and Grandpa are obviously in a fight."

"Yeah?"

"One that they probably wouldn't want us to see."

"Hey, we stumbled in here completely innocently. We came for dinner as usual, per their request, we had no idea we were walking into *The Lion King* without the puppet heads."

Grandpa reappeared at the top of the stairs, this time with Grandma right on his heels holding out a small tape recorder. "Get that out of my face," Grandpa said.

"Just say the tea thing again." Grandma requested.

"You are acting like a child," Grandpa retorted.

"Turn around when you talk, would you? I'm not

sure how good this microphone is," Grandma continued.

Then Grandpa noticed us. "Oh."

"What?" Grandma turned and saw us.

We all stood there for a moment. Then Mom does
what she does best. She took an uncomfortable moment
and made it her own, busting into applause and calling
out "Brava! Encore! I'm sorry, does Terrence McNally
know about you two? Get me the phone."

Grandma and Grandpa stood there and looked at
each other, a little embarrassed. Mom continued her
routine, now doing the wave. I finally got her to stop and
we proceeded with our evening, but once we stepped
foot out of their house, it was nothing but talk about our
early evening entertainment. All the way home, then
into the house, and then following me to my room, pretending she had a tape recorder to get everything I said.
I eventually got her to stop by pulling out some homework, but then she went to check the answering machine and as fate would have it, there was a message
from Grandpa. He forgot to give me a book, and if I had
a moment, stop by after school to pick it up. His voice, of
course, was all Mom needed to start in on her bit again,
and after she relayed the message to me, she went to get
ready for bed. And while I worked on my paper, I heard
her upstairs doing her Grandma and Grandpa bit.

Mom had an early morning meeting on Monday, so we
met at Luke's for breakfast. I wanted her to read my es-
say before I turned it in, so I handed it over and waited.
And waited. I was really nervous about this paper and
her zero reaction wasn't making it any easier on me.
She must hate it. Why wasn't she saying anything? I
couldn't take it anymore.

"Well?" I finally asked.

"Hold on," Mom said as she continued reading.

"It sucks. I know it sucks. Tell me it sucks," I said.

Mom put the paper down and smiled broadly at me. "It's great."

"No, it's not."

"It's an A."

"Don't lie."

"A-plus."

"You're my mom."

"Is anything higher than an A-plus?"

"You have to say that."

"It's an A-plus with a crown and a wand."

"This is not how you raise a child. You don't send them out there with a false sense of pride. Because out there in the real world no one will coddle you. I'd rather know right now if I'm gonna be working at CNN or carrying a basket around its offices with sandwiches in it."

"Rory!" Mom interrupted.

"Yeah?"

"It's great," Mom repeated sincerely.

I smiled. "Really?"

"Really, really," she replied.

"Thank you." I took the paper back from Mom as Luke rushed over to hastily fill our coffee mugs.

"Coffee. Coffee. Okay, what do you want? Eggs? Toast? Combo?" Luke said quickly.

"Whoa. What's the rush, Zippy?" Mom asked.

"I'm just swamped this morning, I was supposed to have"—Luke glanced upstairs toward his apartment—"help, but I don't, so order right now or I'm bringing you both an egg white omelet with a side of steamed spinach."

"Pancakes," Mom said quickly.

"French toast," I added, equally fast.

"Thank you." Luke continued down the counter filling coffee cups. Jess came down the stairs and Luke went up to him, looking at his watch. "Jess, you were supposed to be down here at—" Then he noticed what Jess had on—a fairly horrifying Metallica T-shirt with a huge skull and crossbones. "What the hell is that?"

"What?"

"That."

"That is a shirt."

"Change."

"What?"

"Go upstairs and change that shirt."

"I like this shirt."

"How can you like that shirt?"

"It brings out my eyes."

"This is a diner. People eat here."

"Okay, hold on, hold on . . ." Jess took a pad of paper and a pen out of his back pocket and started writing. "This is a diner, people eat here. Okay. Good to know. Go on."

Luke grabbed the paper and pen from Jess. "Hey! Part of the deal of you staying here is that you work here and when you work here you will wear proper work attire and that is not proper work attire. Now go upstairs and change into something that's not going to scare the hell out of my customers."

"Whatever you say, Uncle Luke," Jess said as he went back upstairs.

"Gross T-shirt," Mom said.

"Yep," I replied.

"Good band," Mom commented.

"Oh yeah," I agreed as we sipped our coffees and waited for our breakfasts.

∽

After school, I headed to Grandma and Grandpa's to pick up the book. A new maid answered the door and showed me to the patio, where Grandma was meeting with her Daughters of the American Revolution group.

"Oh, Rory. What a nice surprise," Grandma said.

"Hey, Grandma. Sorry to butt in like this."

"Nonsense. Come and meet my friends. Ladies, I'd like you to meet my granddaughter, Rory." And she introduced me to Vivian, Natalie, and Sunny.

"My goodness, what a pretty girl you are," Natalie said.

"She looks just like Lorelai, doesn't she?" Sunny added.

"The eyes . . ." said Natalie.

"The nose . . ." said Vivian.

"Walk around, sweetie," Sunny asked.

"Sunny, leave the girl alone," Grandma said.

"I just wanted to see the walk. Lorelai had such a specific walk," Sunny continued.

"Fast," Vivian added.

"That was it," Sunny agreed.

"Come, sit, would you like some tea?" Grandma asked.

"Oh no. I just came to pick up a book that Grandpa was supposed to leave for me."

"Go check his study. It might be on his desk," Grandma said.

"Okay. Thanks." I went back inside, found the book where Grandma suspected it was, and headed back out to the patio to say goodbye.

"I found it," I said, holding the book up. Grandma and her DAR group all turned and stared at me, smiling broadly. That made me unbelievably uncomfortable. "Yay," I added weakly.

"Rory, would you come out here for a moment?" Grandma asked.

"Okay," I said a little suspiciously as I walked over to their table. The ladies made room for me and I sat down. Then they proceeded to tell me about the upcoming Daughters of the Daughters of the American Revolution Debutante Ball and how important it was to be presented to society. Grandma was getting more and more excited as they spoke, and I couldn't turn her down when she asked if I wanted to be involved. So I'm coming out. I've accepted it; the hard part will be telling my mom.

# ∞4

When I got home, Mom was in the kitchen doing homework for the weekly business class she takes. On the bus ride home, I had flipped through some of the DAR brochures Grandma had given me and I realized there really was no good way to get this kind of news out so I went into the house and made my announcement. "I'm coming out."

"Out of what?" Mom said, not looking up from her books.

"Out into society," I replied, walking over to the kitchen table. Mom kept studying.

"What are you talking about?"

"Well, after school I go to Grandma's house . . ." I said, slipping off my backpack and sitting at the table next to Mom. That got her to look up.

"Okay, right away bad," Mom said.

"And her DAR friends are all there and they're talking about this debutante ball that's being thrown . . ."

"Oh no," Mom said with a look of dismay.

"And when I got back from Grandpa's office, they all invited me out onto the patio . . ."

"No, no, no!" Mom grabbed my hand. "Tell me you did not go out onto the patio."

"I went out onto the patio," I stated.

"Oh, Rory, that's like accepting the position as the drummer in Spinal Tap."

"Before I knew it, Grandma was telling me how important it is for a person to be properly presented to society."

"Uhhh . . ." Mom said, making a face.

"And how every young girl dreams of this day . . ."

"Ahhh . . ."

"And how there are flowers . . ."

"Oh Lord . . ."

"And music . . ."

"Please . . ."

"And cake . . ."

"Oh yeah," Mom said, perking up for a second, "the cake's actually good."

"And before I knew it, Grandma was bringing out your old dress and I was trying it on and—"

Mom got up and headed for the phone.

"What are you doing?"

"I am getting you out of this," she said as she started dialing.

"Mom, wait . . ."

"I swear, there is nothing in the world my mother is better at than getting someone to agree to something that in any other universe they would never ever consider."

"Mom . . ."

"I am still convinced that she had something to do with Lily Tomlin doing that movie with John Travolta."

I took the phone away from her. "I'm doing this."

"Why?"

"Because you should have seen the look on Grandma's face when she asked me. It's really, really important to her."

"But—"

"No. If it's that important to her, and it's not that important to me, then why shouldn't I do it?"

"Rory, do you know what a coming out party says?"

"It says I'm a woman now."

"No. It says, 'Hi, I'm Rory. I'm of good breeding and marriageable age and I will now parade around in front of young men of similarly good breeding and marriageable age so they can all take a good long look at me.'"

"You're exaggerating."

"No, it's like animals being up for bid at the county fair, except sheep don't wear hoop skirts."

"Look, I promised. But you don't have to be a part of it if you don't want to."

"No. No. If you want to do it, I'll help. It's just weird. This is all the stuff that I ran away from, I just . . . assumed you'd be running with me."

"Well, I would but I heard debutantes don't run. Something about the heels."

Mom smiled at me. "You sure about this?"

"I figure I'll just look at it as a sociological study. Maybe I can even write a story about it for *The Franklin*."

"All right then, if you're sure . . . Where do we start? Well, let's see," Mom said as we sat back down at the table. "You have a dress, you'll need a dowry, I guess." She plunked a coffee creamer in the shape of a cow down in front of me. "There you go. And you need shoes, hose, gloves, some mice, a dog, a pumpkin . . ."

We both picked up a brochure from the pile Grandma had sent home with me and started perusing it for guidance. And then I saw it. "What's wrong?" Mom asked, noticing my face.

"Uh, nothing," I lied.

"Rory . . ."

I hesitated a moment, then finally told her. "It just says that your father is supposed to present you at the ceremony."

"Oh." Mom closed her brochure and looked at me.

"Whatever. It's no big deal," I stammered. "I can get someone else to do it. Grandpa, probably."

"Rory . . ."

"Or Taylor."

"Okay . . ."

"Or the cable guy looked pretty friendly last week. Maybe he has a tux."

"Hand me the phone."

"I was kidding about the cable guy," I said as I passed the phone over. Mom took it from me and started dialing.

"What are you doing?" I asked.

"Look, missy, there are plenty of things that should weird you out about coming out, but inviting your father shouldn't be one of them."

Through the phone, I could hear the prerecorded tone and the message announcing the number had been changed.

"Oh . . . gum wrapper," Mom said, gesturing at the tiny scrap of paper on the table next to me. I handed it to her.

"He's not going to come," I said.

"You don't know until you ask," Mom replied, scribbling down the number with the highlighter she had been using to study with.

She dialed that number and got another recording.

"Napkin, napkin," she said. I passed that over and she jotted down the new number, which she then dialed.

"Forget it," I said. "I'm sure he's busy. Or traveling, or—"

Mom held her hand up to hush me when someone actually answered the phone. "Oh, sorry," Mom said into the phone. "I must have the wrong number. I was looking for Christopher Haden." She paused a moment and before she could ask, I handed her a full-sized pad of paper. "Fancy," she said as she took it, then wrote yet another number down. "Thanks," she said into the phone and hung up. Then she dialed again.

This was starting to get a little ridiculous. "Mom . . ."

"Look, we call, we ask, there's no harm. Trust me. The cable guy's not going anywhere." She perked up when someone answered on the other end. "Ugh, hi! Where the hell are you?" She got up from the table and went into the living room to continue the conversation. I stayed at the table, not really sure how I would feel if Dad said no. I finally heard her say, "Bye," so I went into the living room to hear the verdict.

"Hey, Little Debbie," Mom said, getting up from the couch, "your dad is definitely gonna be there."

"You're kidding."

"No, he's going to walk you down the stairs and turn you in a circle, watch you curtsy, and announce that Rory Gilmore is officially open for business."

"I can't believe it. And he definitely said 'definitely'?"

"Definitely," Mom said with a smile.

"So it's a fifty-fifty chance." I was starting to get excited.

"I don't know. He sounded pretty sure; I'd say sixty-forty," Mom said, putting her arm around me as we walked back to the kitchen.

⟠

The debutante ball quickly became the main focus of our lives, mostly because Grandma called every other second about it. From those pamphlets, I discovered that in addition to my dad, I needed another escort for the evening, and it only seemed appropriate that that person be my boyfriend, Dean Forrester. Coming to that conclusion was the easy part. Trying to convince him to do something that would force him to wear a tux, well, that would take some work. After a little negotiating, he agreed, and to reinforce my case, I asked him and Lane to come over and watch a video with me.

Mom was pacing around the house, on the phone with Grandma for the eighty-seventh time that day, and we were in the living room watching the tape. I was sitting on the armrest, Dean next to me on the couch, Lane beside him. I turned to Dean. "So?"

"So what?" Dean replied.

"It's good, huh?" I said, motioning to what we were watching.

"It's the Rock and Roll Hall of Fame induction," he stated.

"Yes. And doesn't Neil Young look cool?" I said enthusiastically.

"I guess," he responded halfheartedly.

"If you'll notice, he's wearing a tux," I continued.

Wasn't working. "Neil Young looks cool because he's Neil Young, not because he's wearing a tux," Dean said.

Mom wandered back into the living room, still on the phone. ". . . No, I don't have to ask her, Mom, because I know the answer. I know the answer, Mom, I know the answer. Yeah . . . No . . . Okay, well I don't have to ask her, Mom . . . hold on." Then she turned to me and asked if I wanted Grandma's hairstylist to set my hair before the ball. I looked at her, horrified, and she went back to the phone. "Oh, I did not coach her, Mom. Go back to talking about gloves . . ." And she walked out of the room again.

"I think you're gonna look great in a tux," I said, turning back to Dean.

"Tails," Lane added as she flipped through one of the DAR brochures. Dean quickly looked at Lane to make sure she wasn't kidding, then turned to me, surprised. "What?"

"Yeah," Lane continued, "it says here all escorts must be properly attired in black tails, white cummerbunds, and white gloves."

"What?" Dean said again, now bordering on upset.

"I'm sure the gloves are optional," I said, trying to calm him down.

"Not according to this." Lane held up the pamphlet.

"Tails? Gloves?" Dean repeated.

"Remember Neil Young," I said. Dean just looked at me. "Remember that you love me." Still with the staring and no words. "Remember that I'll be watching *Battlebots* with you for a month."

Dean sighed. "Show me Neil Young again," he said.

As I rewound the tape, a car honked repeatedly in the driveway. "Dad!" I jumped up and ran out the door, my mom close behind me. "Dad!" I called out again as I raced down the steps and toward my dad, who was standing next to his car.

"Whoa! Hold it right there," Dad said. I stopped, a few feet away from him. "A lady never runs out to meet a gentleman caller who hasn't been announced," he continued.

"Sorry. We haven't tamed my wild ways yet," I said, smiling at him.

"Well, thank God I'm here now," he stated.

I completed my journey and gave him a big hug. "I missed you."

"Me too," he replied.

"Hey!" my mom said, kissing my dad on the cheek. "What is this?" She continued on to my dad's shiny new car.

"What? Oh my God, where did that come from?" my dad said, pretending to be surprised when he turned and faced his Volvo.

"What happened to your bike?" Mom asked.

"Crazy game of key exchange at the car wash," Dad replied with a smile.

"This is a car," Mom continued.

"Yes, it is."

"It has four wheels and a roof, and air bags, and seat belts, and my God, it smells like a forest," she said, leaning into the car from the open driver's side window.

Dad walked around to the back of the car. "Well, I needed more space. I had something big to haul." He pulled a massive box out of the trunk and handed it to me. "I believe this belongs to you."

"*The Compact Oxford English Dictionary*!" I said excitedly as I took the box.

Dad smiled at my reaction. "I promised you I'd get it. I'm just sorry it took so long."

"That's okay," I said. I couldn't take my eyes off it.

"On the bright side, this is the new edition. If I'd gotten you the old one, you wouldn't have the word 'jiggy' in it," Dad continued.

"Thank you! I love it! I'm going to go look things up right now!" I started back to the house when Dad stopped me and pulled a magnifying glass out of his pocket and handed that to me. I ran back to the house to show Lane and Dean my new toy.

*The Compact Oxford English Dictionary* is the one volume version of the twenty-volume *Oxford English Dictionary* (universally acknowledged as the world's greatest dictionary). It lists not only current words and meanings, but antiquated ones as well. Nine pages from the twenty-volume set are reduced and put on one page in the one volume version. The magnifying glass is necessary to read the entries. All true writers own the *OED*.

While we were looking up words, loud metal music, courtesy of the band Rammstein, came blaring from Dad's car. I took the opportunity to use some of my new fancy words and asked them to attenuate the cacophony. Look it up.

Now that I had gotten Dean to accept the tux, it was on to the dancing. There was a formal dance with my escort scheduled at the cotillion, so Dean and I went to Miss Patty's for a dance lesson. She hit the "play" button and Frank Sinatra's recording of "The Way You Look Tonight" came out and we awkwardly tried to waltz or foxtrot or two-step around the room with direction called out by Miss Patty.

"Keep counting in your heads," Miss Patty instructed. "Look each other in the eyes. Dean, are you leading?"

"I have no idea," he replied, frustrated.

"Okay, okay, stop stop stop," Miss Patty said as she turned off the music. "Now remember, one of the most important things in ballroom dancing is to remember to spot, otherwise you're gonna get dizzy. So, what you want to do is you want to pick out something to focus on. I usually like to find a lonely seaman," she said, lowering her voice. "Then, when turning, whip your head around and find your spot again." She demonstrated by twirling around and calling out 'Hello, sailor.' 'Hello, sailor.' 'Hello, sailor.' Now you try it."

"You've got to be kidding me," Dean muttered.

"I think you can do it without the 'Hello, sailor' part," I told him.

"Rory . . ."

"*Battlebots*," I reminded.

"For the rest of your life," he stated.

Miss Patty put the music back on, Dean took me in his arms, and we started from the top.

"Hey, you guys are really improving. Now you're actually facing each other," Mom said as she and Dad came into the studio bearing coffee and muffins.

"Anyone need a break?" Dad asked.

Dean quickly nodded and Miss Patty reluctantly agreed.

"So, how's it going?" Mom whispered as Miss Patty went outside for a smoke.

"Actually, I'm not very good," I confessed.

"Yeah, which is really holding me back, because I'm a natural," Dean added.

"Well, maybe you just need a glittery glove and a really freaky face," Mom said.

"At one point, Miss Patty thought Dean was gonna get hurt, she made me sit in the corner and watch," I told her.

"Hey, nobody puts baby in a corner," Mom said in mock outrage.

"It's not your fault," Dad said, trying to console us. "Ballroom dancing is a wonderfully sexist thing. Any woman can do it. All she needs is a strong male lead. No offense, Dean." He playfully twirled and dipped my mom, who didn't quite follow, and they got a little tangled up. "Well, almost any woman can do it."

"I wasn't ready, I wasn't ready," Mom protested, "I want a do-over."

"Fine." Dad stepped away from Mom, turned on the music, and very cordially asked, "May I have this dance?"

"I don't know," Mom replied as Dad took her in his arms, "do you have a trust fund? Always make sure," she directed toward me.

Dad began waltzing her around the room. They both started laughing, but soon they got into it and as the song played out, they did a really beautiful, perfectly executed sequence of steps. Dean and I looked at each other, amazed. Miss Patty watched from the doorway, finishing up her cigarette. I think even Mom and Dad were a little surprised, and when they finished their dance, we all clapped.

"Okay, I'm adopted," I said.

"Yeah, I'm never going to be able to do that," agreed Dean.

"Nah, you guys just need some practice," Dad encouraged.

"Listen to your father, Rory. Your adorable, adorable father," said Miss Patty.

"C'mon," Mom said, turning to my dad, "let's get you out of here before you become Patty's next husband."

"See you guys later," Dad said. "Bye, Patty," he added flirtatiously.

Miss Patty sighed deeply. "Ohhh, the way you toy with me." And then we returned to our dance lesson.

When Dean and I got home, Mom had ordered an obscene amount of Chinese food, and the cartons were spread out across the coffee table. She said something about "last meal." After we finished eating, Dad tried to show Dean how to maneuver his bow tie while Mom and I picked at the leftovers. Then I polished my toes and Mom demonstrated the skills she had learned during her own proper upbringing by balancing a book on her head and walking around the room eating out of a carton with chopsticks. "See, now, only a lady can gracefully walk around a room with a book on her head while eating Kung Pao Chicken," she informed us. "And a great lady can even spit the peanuts back into the container without anyone noticing."

"Wow," I said, impressed.

"Yeah, well, don't be intimidated. You have to practice and practice to get to my level." She tipped her head and the book slid off into her hand.

"Anyone want the last egg roll?" I asked.

"Uh, no," replied Dean.

I reached over to grab it.

"Hey, where are you going?" Mom interrupted, shooting out her arm to block my path.

"To get the egg roll."

"You're getting the egg roll yourself?"

"Yes."

"No," she reprimanded. "Ladies never get their own egg rolls. Ladies never get their own anything. They don't even get their own ideas," she said, handing me the egg roll.

"Oh boy."

"They just sit helplessly and wait for some young strong man to come by and assist them. They don't step in puddles, they don't step over puddles. They can't even look at puddles. They actually need to be blindfolded and thrown in a sack and carried over puddles."

"Isn't there some moratorium on how long ladies are supposed to talk?" I asked, munching on the egg roll.

"Uh . . . no. Now repeat after me, 'I am completely helpless.'"

Dad finished showing Dean the art of the bow tie. I was still immobile because of my toenails so Dean came over to the couch to kiss me goodbye. "I'll see you at three." He started to turn away but I stopped him and handed him a box. "What's this?"

"Your gloves," I told him.

"I thought you were kidding," Dean said.

"Oh no. Ladies never kid," Mom informed him.

Dean sighed, took the box, and walked out the door.

"I think I'm going to go to bed too," I said, getting up off the couch.

"Do you need help?" Mom asked.

"Nope," I replied.

"Wrong! The correct answer is yes! Ladies need help doing everything!" Mom admonished.

"Good night," I said as I hobbled out, walking awkwardly on my heels.

I brushed my teeth and slipped into bed, working around my still impressionable nails. Mom came in after a moment, pulling a blanket up over me, carefully leaving my pedicured toes exposed. "Did you try Grandma again?" I asked. Grandma had been uncharacteristically quiet, considering the ball was tomorrow, even letting us out of our Friday night meal that evening.

"Still not there," she replied.

"I hope everything's okay."

"I'm sure everything's fine. You'll see. She'll be there watching you and she will be thrilled."

"I hope so."

"Okay, sleep well. Tomorrow, you are a woman. Sunday, you start therapy. And a week from Tuesday, the binge drinking begins."

"Great. You know how I like a schedule." I smiled at her.

" 'Night." Mom turned the light out and went up to her bedroom. I was actually really tired, and though I was a little nervous about the dance, it didn't take me long to fall asleep.

# ∽5

The debutante ball was held in the ballroom of a magnificent historical building. The place was buzzing with energy when we walked in as waiters and staff set up for the evening's festivities. Mom was already dressed, but I had come in jeans, carrying my white dress in a garment bag. I was completely in awe at the sight of the room—it was gorgeous. And a little intimidating.

"Wow, this place is huge. Do I have to walk down those stairs?" I asked eyeing the large staircase leading up to the second floor.

"I'm afraid so. Unless you want to make a really memorable entrance and slide down the banister, which I totally encourage, by the way," she replied.

A stern-looking woman, clipboard in hand, came up to us. "You are—"

"Lorelai Gilmore," I answered.

"Late," she finished.

"Sorry," Mom said. "My fault. Took me a while to get pretty. Not all of us are sixteen anymore, you know what I mean?"

The woman stared at my mother, silent. Guess not. She turned back and addressed me. "You are to head up the stairs. The preparation room is on the right."

"Look for the toxic cloud of Chanel and Final Net," Mom advised.

I followed the stern lady up, glancing back at my mom. She ran her hand from her shoulder all the way down her arm and mouthed "sliiiide" as I headed for the stairs.

The prep area was a dressing room filled with clothing racks, vanity tables, and mirrors with lights around them. The room was already full of debutantes in the midst of getting ready. The debutante organizer gave me the tour. "Hang your dress there, put your makeup on over there. You'll have to make do with a nonlighted mirror. The lighted ones went to the girls that were here before dawn." Then she addressed the group. "Listen up, ladies. Everyone must be beautiful and ready to go by seven-thirty."

Several girls gasped and resumed primping with a vengeance. I hung my dress up, found an empty seat, and sat down next to a girl who was currently being worked on by her hairstylist. I pulled out some lip gloss and carefully applied it, and then I returned it to my jacket pocket. Now that I was done with my makeup, I looked at the girls around me. They all looked like they were about to enter the Miss America contest. I turned to the girl next to me. "I can't believe we have an hour and a half."

"I know," she replied. "I'm never gonna be ready in time. God only knows if the swelling on my nose is gonna go down. I had to go and inherit my father's nose." She turned slightly and glanced at me. "I'm Libby."

"Ror—"

"Which one should I wear?" Libby interrupted, holding up two red lipsticks. "I've thought about it all month, and I cannot decide."

I looked at the colors. They looked exactly the same. "Oh, well . . . that's a tough one."

"I know. This is red red and this is orange red. The wrong one, and I will end up looking like a hooker. Or a teacher," she added fatefully.

"That's a lot of pressure."

"The two minutes you are standing on those stairs tonight will determine your social status for the rest of your life."

"Wow. What if you trip?" I joked lightly.

Libby stared at me in horror.

"I mean, not that you would . . . You wouldn't . . . I might . . . Probably will, actually . . . Could be a really Cirque du Soleil kind of night," I stammered out.

"You should not even joke about stuff like that," she said, turning back to her mirror. "Ow! There's a head under there, you know," she said to her hairstylist.

I decided this was probably a good time to put on my dress so I turned away from Libby and her hair issues and unzipped my garment bag. A couple of minutes later and I was dressed and ready to go. I watched and listened to the girls around me for a little while longer, then I slipped off to a corner, pulled out my cell phone, and called Mom.

"They're tweezing everything," I said when she answered the phone.

"Well, if they try to get you, serpentine," Mom counseled.

"So, did you know they put a spotlight on you when you're announced?" I asked.

"Yep," she replied.

"Which means if I do anything stupid or embarrassing the entire room will see it," I continued.

"I'll blind as many people as I can, but I may not get to everyone," Mom told me.

"Try your best," I said. "I better go. The electric versus Velcro rollers debate is about to heat back up."

Like there needs to be a debate. "Velcro," Mom said.

"I know," I replied. I still had a lot of time before the start of the ball, so after I hung up I pulled the ever-present book out of my bag and started reading. A few minutes later, Libby came over and flashed me her flask.

"Midori Sour?" she offered.

"Oh. No, thanks."

"More for me," she said, sitting down and taking a swig. "At my last coming out, I shared with this girl who couldn't handle her booze. Neon green puke all over her white dress."

"Your last coming out?" I asked.

"Oh, this is my fifth one this year," she informed.

"Wow."

"You know," she continued, "they say four out of five debs marry their escorts."

"Kind of like the dentists with Trident."

"I figured five coming-out balls, five escorts, one of them has to stick, right?"

"Good logic."

"So, is your escort the one?"

"The one what?"

"The one you're going to marry."

"Oh well . . ."

"Is he cute?"

"Yes. He is very cute, but . . ."

"Where are you guys planning to live when you get married?"

"Okay, hold on a sec . . ."

A pretty girl with a huge pink Band-Aid on her face passed by. "Katie, hi!" Libby called out. "Too bad about your face."

"Is it horrible?" Katie asked.

"No. You can hardly tell," Libby reassured her, getting up and grabbing Katie's hand. "Just walk sideways," she suggested in a whisper. They walked off and I returned to my book.

An announcement was finally made for fathers to report to the debutante staging area, and the stern debutante organizer arrived to rush us out of the prep area to the hallway near the top of the staircase. "Okay, I want fathers on the right," she instructed, "debutantes on the left. If you don't know right from left, look at the person next to you."

Dean came up from behind and tapped me on the arm. "Hey. I just wanted to see you before you became a proper lady of society."

"So what do you think?" I asked.

"I think . . . you look like a cotton ball."

"Why, thank you, Jeeves."

"But a really cute cotton ball."

Libby, who had been standing in front of me taking swigs of Midori Sour, came around and joined us. "Oh my God, is this your escort?"

"Yeah, it is," I replied.

"You are totally getting married," she giggled, definitely tipsy, as she walked off.

"What did she say?" Dean asked.

"Oh. Well . . ." I faltered, trying to explain. Fortunately, Dad walked in. "Dad, great. Let's go."

"I'll meet you downstairs," Dean said as he headed off. "Good luck."

"Okay," I said, waving the feathered fan I was holding at him. Dad and I took our positions as the announcer asked everyone to take their seats so the presentation could begin.

"Last chance to shimmy down the drainpipe," Dad told me.

"Do me a favor?" I asked.

"Anything."

"Just don't let me fall."

"Right back at ya." Dad smiled, offered his arm, and we were ready to go.

The lights dimmed and people took their seats. A former debutante walked to the podium and started the evening. I scanned the room and found Mom sitting at a table by herself. I wondered where Grandma and Grandpa were.

"Now, the word 'debutante' comes from the French word 'debuter,' which means 'to lead off,'" the presenter continued, "and we hope that tonight will lead off a lifetime of civic responsibility and social awareness for these exceptional young women."

Mom kept glancing off to the side. It was hard to see with all the lights, but it looked like Grandma and Grandpa were standing there. She finally got up and approached them, then grabbed their arms and led them out to the side room. Where were they going? The orchestra began "Thank Heaven for Little Girls" and they started announcing debutantes. I told my dad I was going to get Mom, Grandma, and Grandpa and I headed off.

As I approached the doorway, I heard Grandpa yelling, but I also heard the deb presenter getting closer and closer to "Gilmore." This was my first debutante ball, but I guessed not being in your place when your name is called and the spotlight is thrown on you doesn't win you any points in society. I informed them I was up next and rushed back to my dad just as the deb presenter announced "Elizabeth Doty, daughter of George Edward Doty the Fourth and Eleanore Doty." A somewhat tipsy Libby struggled a little, but her father valiantly kept her upright.

"Lorelai Gilmore, daughter of Christopher Haden and Lorelai Gilmore," came the announcement.

The spotlight hit my dad and me and we made our way down the stairs. Stairs that seemed to go on forever. We finally got to the bottom and my dad kissed my hand. I did a little curtsy as my dad looked to Dean, who was standing off to the side. Dean came over, my dad walked off, and Dean grabbed my hand, tucked it under his arm, and escorted me to my next destination, the Fan Dance. I hoped Mom, Grandma, and Grandpa made it back in time to see this.

The formal dance with Dean went surprisingly well — I think Miss Patty would have been proud — and finally the evening came to an end.

On the drive back to Stars Hollow, Mom told me Grandpa thought he was being phased out of his company. That's what Grandma and Grandpa had been arguing about when we went to dinner at their house and that's what the yelling was on the patio that evening. I felt awful. Grandpa had been with his company for thirty years and loved his job. I really hoped he was wrong.

We met Dad and Dean back in town, and Dad and I walked side by side, Mom and Dean behind us, down the streets of Stars Hollow. "So, did you know that you're considered a hot dad?" I said.

"Really?" Dad asked.

"Libby said that it's too bad you're my real dad, because if you were my stepdad, I could steal you away from Mom," I told him.

"That Libby's got a good life ahead of her," Dad replied.

"Well, I was very proud of all of you," Mom said. "You made it through the entire ceremony with a completely straight face. Almost all of you," she directed toward my dad.

"I'm sorry, but that Fan Dance was more than I could take."

"Hey, I need a burger," Mom announced.

"Me too," I said. "Dean?"

"Honestly, the only thing I can think of is taking off this tux," Dean replied.

"Hey, watch it. You're talking to a lady, now," Mom reminded him.

"Well, how about if I do it at home?" Dean asked.

"Better," Mom said.

"Thanks again for going with me," I said to Dean.

"Tomorrow you start paying." He kissed me and then headed home. Dad had to leave early the next morning, so he decided to call it a night too.

"What? Not even time for fries?" I asked.

"I tell you what. I'll get up a little early and have coffee with you before I go. Deal?"

"Deal." I gave him a hug.

Mom asked me to go ahead and order, so I went on to Luke's, leaving Mom and Dad to talk.

The diner was quiet, and Luke brought my burger and fries quickly. I was just about to bite into my burger when Mom walked in.

"Hey," Mom called out.

I froze, burger mid-air. "What?"

"After all you've been through tonight, and I come in here and find you eating like that?"

I thought about what she said for a minute, then stuck out my pinkie finger.

"There you go," Mom said proudly as she sat next to me.

"Being a lady is hard," I told her.

"So, tonight, what's the consensus?"

"The Fan Dance was humiliating. I'm never doing a curtsy again. But having Dad around was great," I said with a smile.

Mom looked a little wistful. "Yeah. It was."

"He's got a new girlfriend, you know."

"Sherry."

"Yeah."

"Poor girl's named after a Journey song. That's gotta be rough."

"He seems happy."

"He does. He really . . . does."

"I'm glad."

Mom paused for a millisecond before agreeing with me.

"I feel kind of bad for Grandma, though. She was so into this night and then she ended up being so miserable . . ."

"Don't worry. She'll have more fun at the next one."

I stared at her. "Excuse me?"

"Yes. We have you signed up for the next six balls."

"Not funny."

"Hey, you're doing this till you bring home a prize."

"Ignoring you now."

Luke came over with Mom's food. "So," he said, setting the plate in front of her, "back from the ball, huh?"

"Yes," Mom replied. "I left behind a glass slipper and a business card in case the prince is really dumb."

"Good and desperate thinking," Luke said.

"Thank you," Mom said proudly. She noticed Jess, who had just come down the stairs behind Luke. "Hmm, Luke?"

"What?" Luke turned and saw Jess, who was wearing a plaid shirt and a baseball cap on backward, looking remarkably like a certain diner owner, wiping down the counter. Luke went up to him. "What do you think you're doing?" he asked.

"Working," Jess replied.

"So, you think this is funny, huh?"

"I'm sorry," Jess answered, gesturing to his clothes. "I thought this was the uniform."

"Okay, you know what? That's fine. Have your little joke. You know, doesn't bother me at all. Just go over there and clean off that table. Okay? I'm ignoring you. You do not exist."

"Okay." Jess walked over to the table and started cleaning it, daintily lifting items to wipe underneath. Luke started wiping down the front counter, trying to ignore him.

"That's it! Get upstairs and change!" Luke exploded.

Jess stopped working. "Whatever you say, Uncle Luke," he said, glancing at me with a small, almost conspiratorial smile. It *was* kind of funny.

"It's Luke! Just Luke! Mr. Luke!" Luke said, following him. "In fact, don't address me at all!" he called up the stairs after Jess. He threw his rag down, frustrated, and headed to the kitchen. Then it was just the two of us, proper ladies in their proper attire, with our burgers and fries.

∽

Mom and I got a lot of mileage out of the debutante ball, referring to the days preball as the Days Before I Knew Better, and after the ball, Mom would say "That is the only and correct response for a lady of society" to *everything* I said. But soon, school and life got back to the Days Before I Knew Better and here I was singing a Barry Manilow song at Luke's. Before you judge, you must hear why. We were once again at Luke's for breakfast. And really, I hope you've realized by now that there's no other place to go, Luke's is simply the best. It was pretty full when we walked in. "Wow," Mom said, "busy today. Has Luke been advertising or something?"

"He gets good word-of-mouth," I replied as we headed for the last available table.

"Well, we've got to start spreading bad word of mouth so we always have a table."

"Well, that would be wrong, but sure. Vermin?" I suggested as we sat down.

"Or no potable water," Mom replied

"Or no potable vermin," I added.

"That would scare them away."

"Or confuse them away."

We looked over at Luke, who was chatting with an elderly Stars Hollow resident.

"It's so weird to see him talking like that," Mom said.

"Like what?" I asked.

"Just all friendly. He's usually only good for a quick couple of gruff monosyllables, and then he's off."

"He is the master of the monosyllable," I agreed.

"He never flirts with any of the women. Do you notice that?"

"He's flirted with you numerous times."

"Don't start."

"Hey, flirt with him now. We need coffee."

"Oh, Luke!" Mom called out, doing her best Scarlett O'Hara, "we're just dyin' for some refreshments!" She waved a napkin like a hanky for effect.

"Keep your pants on," Luke said gruffly.

"Huh, he can turn it off and turn it on so fast," Mom said.

"Hey, I found a CD under the front seat of our car. Did you lose one?" I asked innocently. Now typically, hoarding of any music is frowned upon in the Lorelai Gilmore/Lorelai Gilmore household. But in this case I was okay with it.

"Not that I know of," Mom answered, "but I'm kind of sloppy with them."

"So you didn't hide it?"

"Why would I hide a CD?"

"I don't know. Bay City Rollers . . ."

"It is not a Bay City Rollers CD."

"How do you know?" I asked quickly.

"Because I know what's not hidden under that seat," Mom said, a little defensively.

"Ha! Because you know that Barry Manilow's under that seat."

"Ohhh," Mom grimaced, caught.

"Where's Barry Manilow?" Luke asked, approaching with the coffeepot.

"Under Mom's seat," I replied.

"Sure. Where else would he be?" Luke said.

"All right, I confess, I was hiding Barry Manilow."

"You confess!" I was thrilled.

"But he was very big when I was very small. And it's the live version where he does a medley of all the commercial jingles he's written," Mom explained.

"Don't worry. Everyone's allowed a guilty pleasure now and again," I told her.

"Very diplomatic from the girl who had the Bryan Adams poster above her bed for two years," Mom said.

"Fink."

"Do you have a guilty pleasure, Luke?" Mom asked.

"Nah," Luke said.

"Are you into music?" Mom asked.

"Sure," Luke replied.

Mom turned to me. "Monosyllabic Man strikes again."

"We'll have two muffins, please," I said to Luke.

"You got it." And he walked away.

I started giggling.

"What?" Mom asked.

I kept giggling. "Oh, Barry Manilow . . ."

"Stop," demanded Mom.

"Looks like we made it . . ." I sang.

"Oh yeah? Spice Girls . . ."

"Duran Duran . . ."

"Dido . . ."

"Olivia Newton-John."

"The Macarena. You and Lane. For hours and hours. For weeks on end." Mom demonstrated.

"Hey, we were mocking! You can't mock the mocking!" I stated.

"All right, this is getting ugly, let's stop."

"Let's be friends again."

"All right." And we picked up our coffee cups and clinked them together to seal the deal. But I couldn't help it. Once "Copacabana" starts going through your head, it won't go away. But we had clanked the sacred coffee mugs, so I held all the many ways to teasing Mom about Barry Manilow inside and just giggled and giggled while Mom glared at me.

# ∽6

Monday was soon upon us again and I was in the kitchen grabbing some juice before heading for the bus stop. Mom, who had said goodbye a few minutes earlier, came back in through the kitchen door."Aggggh," she said, frustrated.

"What?" I asked.

"The car won't start."

"What happened?"

"I don't know. It's just dead. I turn the key, and it makes this horrible sound."

"What kind of sound?"

Mom gave me her version of what a battery on its last legs might sound like and added, "You know, but less feminine."

"That's the battery," I told her as I moved to the table and started putting my books into my backpack.

"Well, what did I ever do to make my battery mad?"

"Let's see . . . you've kept the radio on all night, killing the battery, you've kept the lights on all night, killing the battery, you've kept the door open which keeps the ceiling light on all night, killing the battery . . ."

"Okay, well I've done multiple things to make my battery mad."

"Are you going to walk?" I asked as I propped my backpack up, hoping that would shift all the contents to the bottom so I could fit more things in there.

"I'm wearing heels."

"Change your shoes."

"I'd have to change my outfit."

"Change your outfit."

"I'd have to walk upstairs."

"Suddenly I'm living with Zsa Zsa Gabor."

"I'll gonna call Michel." Mom picked up the phone and dialed the inn for Michel, the concierge at the inn, while I tried to fit one more book into my already completely overstuffed backpack.

"This thing is too small," I said, frustrated. I took some books out, rearranging yet again.

"Hold on, Michel," Mom said into the phone. "That backpack is not too small," she told me.

"It's minuscule," I replied, trying another configuration to see if I could get everything to fit.

"Just take your schoolbooks and leave some of the other books," Mom suggested.

"I need all my other books."

"You don't need all of them."

"I think I do."

"The Edna St. Vincent Millay?" she asked, holding the book up.

"That's my bus book."

"Uh huh." She picked up another book off the table. "What's the Faulkner?"

"My other bus book."

"So just take one bus book."

"The Millay is a biography and sometimes if I'm on the bus and I pull out a biography and I think to myself, Well, I don't really feel like reading about a person's life right now, then I'll switch to the novel and sometimes if I'm not into the novel, I'll switch back."

Mom moved on. "What is the Gore Vidal?"

"Oh. That's my lunch book."

"Uh huh. So lose the Vidal or the Faulkner. You don't need two novels."

"Vidal is essays."

"But the Eudora Welty's not essays," she said, holding up that book. "Or a biography."

"Right."

"So it's another novel. Lose it."

"It's short stories," I explained, taking it from her and adding it to my pack.

"This is a sickness," Mom said as she went back to the telephone. She negotiated a ride with Michel while I continued to struggle with my backpack. As she hung up, I managed to successfully zip up my bag.

"Ha! I made it all fit," I said, patting the bag, quite satisfied. "Edna, Bill, Gore, and Eudora, all safe and sound." I lifted the bag off the table and put it on my back.

"Cool," Mom said. Then she pointed to a shelf behind me. "That's your French book."

"Huh?" I turned around and saw the book. "Oh. I know," I said, picking it up, "I'm, um, *carrying* my French book," I covered as I started for the front door.

"Mm hmm, you so thought that French book was already in there," Mom said, grabbing my jacket as she followed me.

"I did not."

"You have a problem."

"No, I don't," I said, taking my coat from her and speeding ahead to get away.

"You're gonna tip over backwards from the weight of that backpack," she continued.

"No, I'm not," I insisted, walking out the door.

"I'm going to have to buy you a forklift!" she called out after me.

Hey, she can say whatever she wants. A girl needs her options.

My morning classes went quickly and soon it was lunchtime at Chilton. I headed for the dining room with my food tray, which held all my essentials: sandwich, soda, book, and portable CD player. I walked to my usual fairly empty table and set my things down. Then I sat, put on my headphones and hit the "play" button. "Know Your Onion" by the Shins blared through my ears as I popped open my soda and pulled out Gore Vidal's essays. I opened it to the proper page, grabbed my sandwich, and happily started reading and eating. A second later, someone tapped me on my shoulder, surprising me. A woman stood over me.

"I startled you," she said. "I didn't mean to."

"That's okay. I'm easily startled," I replied.

"I'm Mrs. Berdinis, a guidance counselor. Your name's Rory, isn't it? Rory Gilmore?"

"Yes. Hello." I awkwardly extended my hand.

"Hello," Mrs. Berdinis said, shaking my hand. "I'd love to sit and talk to you. Can we do that?"

"Sure," I replied. "Anytime."

"How about after you finish your lunch?"

"Oh. That soon?" I said, confused.

"I think soon would be good."

"Okay. What's this about?"

"We'll talk about it then."

I smiled at her. "Not even a hint?"

"See you in a little bit," Mrs. Berdinis said as she walked away.

"Right." I turned back to my book and food, and put on my headphones, but it was hard to enjoy lunch not knowing why the guidance counselor wanted to talk to me, and I ate the rest of my lunch a little distracted.

Mom was sitting on the porch reading a magazine when I got home from school. I sat next to her, dejected, and told her what happened with Mrs. Berdinis.

As requested, after lunch I went to her office. She told me not to worry about being late for my next class; she would write a note if I was. Then she started leafing through a folder, telling me she knew I was a stickler for punctuality from my records.

"I am a stickler, yes," I replied. "I only slipped one time last year. I hit a deer."

"A deer?" she asked.

"He actually hit me. Or she did. Or not me, my car. But then he or she ran away. But I think it turned out okay. I didn't see it again, so I can't definitively say, but I did look for him. Or her." I sighed. "It's a big story for me, I'm surprised I don't tell it better."

Mrs. Berdinis proceeded to tell me why she had called me into her office. Headmaster Charleston had called me to her attention a few weeks prior. He was concerned, and she was as well after observing me for a bit.

"You've been observing me?" I asked.

"We've been concerned about your social behavior here at school," she replied.

"What about it?"

"You don't seem to interact much with the other students."

"I do sometimes. In class, all the time."

"But rarely outside of class. At lunch, you're always by yourself."

"That's when I catch up on my reading," I explained.

"And that Walkman. It makes you very unapproachable," she continued.

"You approached me," I said.

"And you almost jumped out of your skin. What does that tell you?"

"That I'm jumpy," I stated plainly. "On the Fourth of July, forget it, I'm a wreck. And when the Stars Hollow orchestra begins to play in the gazebo, the guy banging the cymbals . . . drives me nuts."

"Denying your problem doesn't solve a problem, Rory. Unless something changes, this could affect your future."

"But I don't understand. I get good grades. Isn't that enough?"

She said it wasn't and went on to tell me when they make recommendations to universities on behalf of the student, that student's social skills are a big part of that. Neither universities nor Chilton look kindly on loners.

"But I'm not a loner," I protested. "Loners are those guys that you see walking around wearing, I don't know, out-of-date clothing, bell bottoms, and they tend to carry a duffel bag with God knows what inside. That's a loner."

"Loners come in all shapes and sizes," Mrs. Berdinis responded. "Even pretty girls."

I sighed, lost for words. Then she told me to try and improve, mix it up with others, maybe start with lunch.

"I don't suppose there's a lunchtime-reading-slash-Walkman-listening club I could join, is there?" I joked. She didn't find that funny.

Mom was miffed by the whole thing. "So what does she expect you to do?"

"She said 'mix it up,'" I replied.

"Mix it up? What does that mean?"

"I guess that means going up to strange kids at school and saying, 'Hey, mind if I awkwardly butt in where I don't belong and don't want to be?'"

"The whole thing's ridiculous. Chilton is a cult."

"Lorelai?" Kirk, Stars Hollow's jack-of-all-trades called out.

"Hold on," Mom said as she got up and walked to the driveway where Kirk's legs were sticking out from underneath the Jeep.

"What is it, Kirk?"

"Big problem, here. Big problem."

"Great. What is it?"

"I'm stuck."

"That's the problem?"

"A very big problem. I'm losing circulation. Could you give me a tug?"

Mom pulled on his legs, dislodging him, and he rolled out. "Man, it's gross under there."

"You find a problem with the car yet, Kirk?"

"Nope, but I'm honing in."

Mom came back and sat next to me, continuing our conversation. "You get great grades. Did you tell her you get great grades?"

"Apparently that's not enough," I told her.

"Hey, Lorelai," Kirk interrupted again. "Do you

know what this is?" He held up a car part by its attached cables.

"Uh, no," she called back.

"Damn." He went back to work on the car.

"I don't know," I said, dejected. "Maybe there is something wrong with me."

"Oh, don't say that."

"Maybe I am a loner. I mean, you were mocking my backpack today. I might just be one step away from carrying a mysterious duffel bag."

"Oh no. No you don't. Don't you go doubting who you are or how you should be. How dare that woman do this to you!" Mom said, upset.

"It wasn't just her. The whole meeting was Charleston's suggestion."

"Well, good. It's time I called on old Snickelfritz Charleston to tell him to stop messing with my kid's mind."

"Mom . . ."

"No. I'm sorry. I don't like this. Schools like Chilton try to stamp out every vestige of individuality and I'm not gonna let that happen."

"It's all fixed," Kirk said, coming over to the porch. "I found a loose terminal. I reconnected the battery and jumped it so it's set to go."

"Oh, thanks, Kirk," Mom replied.

"And I'm not going to charge you for the time I spent stuck underneath the car."

"That's great, Kirk."

"And I just want you to know that I overheard, and you're absolutely right. I carried a duffel bag and ate lunch by myself my entire school career and I turned out just fine," Kirk said as he walked away.

Mom and I looked at each other. "Well, I'm still go-

ing down there," she told me as we headed into the
house.

☙

We agreed to meet at Chilton after Mom's meeting with
Headmaster Charleston, but she never came by. I
checked in his office but his secretary, Mrs. Traiger,
said Mom had already left. That was weird. I took the
bus back to Stars Hollow and walked home. I found her
sitting at the kitchen table drinking coffee and staring at
a piece of paper. I stopped in the doorway to the
kitchen. "Hey!"

"Hey," Mom answered, distracted and still staring at
the sheet.

I was stunned. "Hey!" I said again, as I walked to the
table and took my backpack off.

"Yeah, look, Fat Albert, get me a soda, will you?"

"Mom, what are you doing here? You were supposed
to meet me at my Latin class after meeting with Headmaster Charleston," I reminded, sitting at the table next
to her.

Mom looked up at me. "Oh God, I was. I totally forgot. I'm so sorry."

"Mom, come on, what happened? Did you talk to
him?"

"I did. I told him that he was completely out of line
with his treatment of you. That you are not a loner
freak, you have plenty of friends and do not own a long
black leather Matrix coat and they should fall down on
their knee socks every day that you even deign to show
up at that loser school."

"And?"

"And then he yelled at me."

"He what?"

"He pulled out a file and told me I was a bad Chilton mom."

"He did not."

"And that I don't participate in school activities."

"But you work."

"And I don't make posters . . ."

"You have no artistic capabilities."

"And I don't chaperone school dances."

"Does he know you got pregnant at sixteen?"

"Basically, I'm not doing my part to help further your educational future."

"So, we both got busted."

"Yes."

"Great."

"Now, I have to pick a group or a cause or sponsor a club or something . . ." Mom said, indicating the list she had been staring at.

"This sucks."

Mom put down the list and smiled at me. "But hey, I've been thinking, we did this whole Chilton thing to get you into Harvard, right?"

"Right," I agreed tentatively.

"And these fanatics that run your school, they're the ones that write the letters to the fancy colleges saying things like, 'Hey, she's keen, look at her,' or 'Have you seen the 'L' tattooed on her forehead 'cause it sure is a big one.'"

"So, you're saying we should just go along with this?"

"Yeah. Go along with it. Talk to some kids, I'll hang out with their moms, and we'll get into Harvard, take over the world, and buy Chilton and turn it into a rave club. What do you say, deal?"

"Deal," I agreed.

We smiled at each other, resigned, then glanced down at the list of potential clubs for Mom.

"Ooh, look," she said, "the Chilton Cheer Society wear matching hats. Eh?" She looked at me. "Go Harvard," she added disconsolately, dropping the list.

# ⌂7

The next day at lunch, I walked into the fairly full Chilton dining room and headed to my regular table. I set my tray down, and then I remembered the deal. I looked around and spotted a lively-ish table of chatting girls. I took a deep breath, picked my tray back up, and walked over to them.

"Hey," I said, interrupting their conversation. All the girls at the table turned and looked at me.

"Hey," responded the girl sitting at the end closest to me. She had short red curly hair.

"There's a bad draft over there where I usually sit. It's kind of like a big downward gust. It's not exactly 'Toto, we're not in Kansas anymore' but it's still pretty darn uncomfortable. Especially when you've just gotten your hair to behave."

The girls looked at each other, a little confused and slightly amused.

"So . . ." I continued, "can I sit here?"

"Uh . . . yeah," the same girl replied.

"Thanks." I set down my tray and sat at the empty

spot across from her. The other girls sized me up. "Nice table," I noted. "It's much more level than over there."

"Your name is Lorry," said the girl who had been talking to me.

"Rory," I corrected.

"Right. Rory."

"What's yours?" I asked.

"Francie," answered the dark-haired girl sitting next to her.

"You're Francie?" I asked the dark-haired girl.

"No. She's Francie," she replied, motioning to the red-haired girl. "I'm Ivy."

"Francie's spokesman," I observed.

Francie smiled at me before replying. "Well, I am a very important person. And everyone knows very important people never speak for themselves."

"I did not know that. But I do now," I told her.

Francie introduced the rest of the girls. "That's Azure, Lily, Celine, Lana, Asia, Anna, and Lem."

"Lem," I repeated, turning to the girl next to me.

"Short for Lemon," Lem explained.

"Oh, sure," I said.

"We were just discussing homecoming. Thoughts?" Francie asked.

"Great movie. Oh wait. That was *Coming Home*. Sorry."

The girls smiled and so did I. Paris walked past the table as Francie said, "I truly believe the whole homecoming dance ritual should be put to sleep."

"Or at least assigned a new color scheme," Ivy added.

Paris backed up, a look of horror on her face, then she quickly walked away.

"Rory, huh? Do they call you Ror?" Francie asked.

"Not unless provoked," I replied.

"No nickname?" Ivy wanted to know.

"Actually, Rory is a nickname," I answered. "My full name's Lorelai."

"Lorelai. That's a weird name," said Lemon.

I turned and looked at her. "Well, Lem, what can I say?"

"It sounds Southern," Francie said. "Are you a belle?"

Just then the bell signaling the end of lunch rang.

"No. But apparently I command them."

"Well, see you later, Your Highness," Francie said as the girls all got up to leave. I breathed a sigh of relief and smiled. That was okay. I gathered my things together, put my lunch tray away, and headed to class.

As I walked through the crowded hallway, Paris suddenly appeared.

"God!" I said, startled. "You're like a pop-up book from hell!"

"You were sitting with the Puffs! How did you do it?" Paris demanded.

"The who?" I asked.

"The Puffs! The Chilton Puffs! You were at their table and I want to know how!" Paris was bordering on hysterical.

"I don't know. I just . . . sat down," I told her.

"Nobody just sits down with them. You have to be invited."

"Paris, it's not the Costa Nostra."

"No. They're the Puffs! The most influential sorority at Chilton."

"Chilton has sororities?"

"Only ten worth mentioning and the Puffs? They have been number one for at least the last fifty years. My mother was a Puff. My aunt was a Puff . . ."

"I thought only colleges had sororities."

"And the connections you make in the Puffs, they last the rest of your life. My cousin Maddie got her internship at the Supreme Court because of Sandra Day O'Connor."

"Sandra Day O'Connor was a Puff?"

"Yes! She was Puffed in 1946, became the president in '47, and in '48 she actually moved the group to the very table you sat at today."

"God."

"It was quite a controversial move at the time but she was just that powerful."

"I had no idea."

"What did you say about me?" Paris asked nervously.

"What?"

"Did you tell them you hated me?"

"I didn't mention you."

"Because I have been killing myself trying to get invited in. I spent all of last year sucking up to Francine Jorvis."

"You mean Francie?"

Paris was crushed. "You call her Francie?"

"Oh. No. Someone else did."

Paris continued. "I have helped her with her homework, secured her a prime spot in the parking lot, organized her locker, scrunched up the plastic strands on her pom-poms to make them fluffy . . . I have done everything except give her a manicure and by God, if I had any talent with an orange stick I would've done that too!"

"I know I'm not the first one to say this to you, but you're insane."

Paris sighed, then softly said, "Okay, look, I know you and me, we —"

"Should not be around each other armed," I finished.

"Yes. But, you have to understand . . . I have to get

into that group. I just . . . have to. My family's name and reputation, not to mention my entire future, all depend on me getting into that group."

"It's just a clique," I told her. "That's all."

"Look, all I'm asking is please don't say anything horrible about me. Don't tell them that you hate me," Paris requested.

"Paris, come on. I'm not in their group. They don't care what I say."

"They let you sit at their table all the way through lunch. You're in."

"Paris . . ." I said, trying to bring her back down to earth with the rest of us.

"You know what, never mind. Do what you want. I don't care." And she walked off. I looked after her, not fully understanding why she was so upset.

Mom picked me up after school and I told her about Paris and the Puffs as we drove to my grandparents' house for our weekly dinner.

"Who the hell names their kid Lemon?" Mom asked as we got out of her car.

"Someone really into citrus," I answered as we headed for the front door.

"Ugh, crazy, crazy people," Mom said, shaking her head.

"It's just so weird that the one table I sit down at is home to this secret society."

"I know. It's like waking up one day and realizing that everyone else in your family can pull their face off." Mom rang the doorbell.

"Yes," I replied. "It's exactly like that." Mom *is* the only one who understands me.

A maid answered the door and informed us we would be barbecuing that night and to head out to the patio. Mom and I looked at each other, surprised and pleased.

"Does Grandma have a barbecue?" I whispered through my teeth as we walked into the house and headed for the patio.

"I don't know," Mom replied quietly. "Maybe she keeps it in that secret room with the paper napkins and the mismatched sheets."

A man in a full chef's uniform was standing at the barbecue grilling things.

"Wow," Mom said, stunned. "She really is barbecuing."

"How cool," I said.

We walked over to see what was on the grill. "What's up, pop and fresh?" Mom said to the chef manning the grill. He smiled at her.

"Ooh, corn," I said, excited.

"Nice," Mom agreed.

We each grabbed an ear of corn off the grill, sat on the bench, and started eating. Grandma came out to the porch and looked at us in horror. "What is this, a refugee camp? Come inside and eat at the table."

"Mom, the whole point of barbecuing is to eat outside," my mom said.

"Animals eat outside. Human beings eat inside with napkins and utensils. If you want to eat outside, go hunt down a gazelle. Make your decision, I'll be inside." And with that, Grandma turned and walked back into the house. Mom and I looked at each other.

"What are the odds of finding a gazelle around here?" Mom asked.

"Slim to none," I replied.

"Okay. Let's go." We got up and joined my grandmother, who was already seated at the table in the dining room.

"I'm extremely disappointed in you, Lorelai," Grandma said when we walked into the room.

"Hold on," Mom told her as she took her jacket off, handed it to the maid, then sat at the table, picking up her napkin and placing it on her lap. "Okay. Go ahead." I handed my jacket to the maid as well, then walked around and sat at my place across from my mom.

Grandma continued. "I had lunch with Bitty Charleston today and she told me what happened with you and the headmaster."

"What? Jeez, does that woman do nothing all day but hide under his desk with a tape recorder?" Mom asked.

"After all we've gone through to get Rory in that school, and then you humiliate us all by not being involved? That's just incomprehensible."

Mom pointed at me, accusingly. "Hey, she wasn't involved either."

"Wow. Just sitting here," I said.

"You are a grown up. You have to set an example. If she's not involved with school then she learned it from you," Grandma reprimanded.

"Yeah," I added.

"How hard is it to help out just once in a while? Join a group, attend a meeting, and all for the sake—" Grandma continued.

"Mom, stop already. Please. I have joined a group, okay?"

"You have?" Grandma said, surprised.

"You have?" I said, equally stunned.

"Yes," Mom replied.

"Which one," Grandma wanted to know.

"I'm going to join the . . . Booster Club. Okay? The Booster Club. I'm going to boost."

Grandma studied Mom for a moment. "Well, the Boosters are a very fine organization."

"That's why I picked them," Mom said, pleased with her last-second choice.

"They do very good work for the school," Grandma continued.

"All went into the picking process," Mom said.

"And the matching sweatshirts they wear are just darling," Grandma finished.

Mom shot me a look, and I tried not to laugh. She looked down at her dinner plate, defeated.

∽

Mom went to her first Boosters meeting a few days later and walked into a room full of ladies discussing a charity fashion show. After introductions were made, Mom told them she managed the Independence Inn and maybe that would be a good place for the affair, adding the inn had one of the greatest chefs in the area. The women were thrilled with the idea and even more excited when Mom offered to organize the event. "I'm sorry, are you from heaven," one of the Boosters asked. Everything was perfect, everyone loved her, and Mom was quite pleased with herself. And then they told her they were all, including her, going to be the models.

I mocked her mercilessly as she told me the story on the way to breakfast the next morning. "Ha ha, yours is worse than mine," I said as we walked down the street.

"Ahhh, they totally just snuck that modeling thing in," Mom said, still upset.

"Hmm, my mom's a model. Maybe you'll get to date Leonardo DiCaprio now," I continued.

"Plus, now I have to plan this whole stupid thing."

"Lorelai Gilmore," I said. "Nope. Doesn't sound model-y enough. You need something that stands out more. How about Waffle? We could call you Waffle and say you're from Belgium."

"Okay. I'm crabby and I need to do something about

it." So she pulled out her cell phone and called Grandma. She told her about the meeting with the Boosters the night before and how she'd volunteered to organize the fashion show. "Yes," Mom went on, "and since I know how concerned you are about how Rory's perceived at Chilton I knew you'd want to be involved somehow so you're going to be one of the models." Mom glanced at me, pleased with herself. She went on to give Grandma the information and though there was resistance at first, Grandma finally agreed.

"You feel better now?" I asked as Mom hung up the phone.

"Waffle is very happy," Mom replied giddily. And we continued on toward Luke's.

∽

Later that day, I walked into the Chilton dining room and went to my usual table. I set the tray down and just as I was taking my backpack off, Francie marched over to me. "Sit with us, please," she said, then walked away.

"Uh . . . okay." I picked up my tray and headed over to Francie's table, setting my tray down once again in the spot across from her.

"Welcome," said Lem.

"We talked, we find you fascinating," Francie said.

"Like the monkey habitat," Ivy added.

"So," Francie continued, "we've decided to extend an invite to you. You can eat here anytime you like."

"Wow. That's nice of you. Thanks," I replied. "Hey, can I ask about this whole sorority thing?"

Francie pretended not to know what I was talking about. "Pardon?"

"Sororit-what?" Ivy added innocently.

"Oh, well, I thought you guys were—" I started.

Lem interrupted. "We have no idea what you're talking about."

"That's right," said Francie. "After all, what's the point of a secret society if it's not secret."

"The whole school apparently knows about it," I explained, noticing as Paris wandered over and lingered behind our table.

"No one has proof. It's just folklore," Francie replied.

"Like Snow White and Rose Red," added Ivy.

"Or Mariah Carey's crack-up," said Francie.

"Have you heard her fan message recently? She's fine and is currently busy staring at a really beautiful rainbow," Lem said.

"Survivor. Hello," Ivy said, obviously.

I glanced over at Paris, who was now leaning against the wall, pretending to read. "Friend of yours?" Francie asked, following my look.

"Paris? Oh, well . . ." I replied.

"Too intense," Ivy said.

"Way too intense," Lem added.

"She comes from a long line of us, though," Francie said.

"I hate nepotism," said Ivy.

"It, however, does make the world go round," Lem remarked.

"You know, Paris, while yes, a little intense, is also very smart," I stated.

"So I drop a box of matches on the floor she can tell me how many there are?" Francie asked.

"She's the editor of the paper, amazing writer, plus funny," I continued.

"She's funny," Ivy said skeptically.

"Oh, yeah. Hilarious. I mean, the times we have

spent laughing together . . . I tell you. The girl's a regular Gary Muledeer," I said.

"She asked you to talk her up, didn't she?" Francie realized.

"No, not at all," I replied.

"Right," Ivy said.

"No. Really. I think she's actually thinking of joining another nonexistent group," I told them.

"What?" Francie said, disturbed.

"But her family is fully Puffed," Ivy stated.

"I don't know. Maybe I heard her wrong but I think that's what I heard her say."

"A voluntary defector," Francie said to Ivy.

"Francie . . ." Ivy warned in a low voice.

"I know," Francie said. She and Ivy turned around. "Paris?" called Francie.

Paris looked at Francie, perplexed. "Yeah?"

"I think the wall can hold itself up just fine, don't you?" Francie asked.

"What?" Paris replied.

"You should sit," Francie suggested.

"Sit?" Paris asked.

"Here," Francie answered, tapping the table.

"Sit there?" Paris was confused.

"Or here," Ivy chimed in.

"Or anywhere for that matter," Lem added.

"Well . . ." Paris wasn't sure what to do.

"Unless you've got somewhere else to be," I prodded. "Another table, perhaps?"

Paris was now truly confused. "Another table?" she echoed.

"No, you have to sit right here." Francie tapped Ivy and everyone in that row slid down a seat. "Come, come," she said as she too moved down a chair.

Paris looked at me and I gave her a little encouraging nod.

"Uh . . . okay," Paris said, "I guess I can sit. For a little while anyhow." She took Francie's old seat across from me. She was so happy she almost smiled. "What did you say?" she mouthed to me. I just smiled and shrugged, then returned to my meal.

The table continued chattering about homecoming and other important issues and I watched a very happy-to-be-included Paris.

School and this new socializing thing kept me busy, and Mom's time was occupied by the upcoming fashion show. Her big day quickly arrived and she headed out to the inn early in the afternoon to make sure everything was running smoothly, which left me with a nice and quiet house. I did laundry, ordered some food, and hung out in my old comfy sweats all day. The perfect Saturday. It was great.

When Mom returned that night, I was settled in on the couch reading one of Simone de Beauvoir's autobiographical books *Memoirs of a Dutiful Daughter*. She looked tired but happy.

"How was it?" I asked.

"Oh, fine," Mom replied. "It ran smoothly, and the food was amazing. Michel only made three people cry."

"And how was the fashion show?"

"Well, you know, I walked up and down the ramp, looked pouty and sexy and now I'm ready for rehab," Mom answered as she headed into the kitchen.

"I brought you some Booster cake," she called out.

"Put it in the fridge, please."

"Okay."

"How was Grandma?"

"She was . . . good," Mom said through a mouthful of cake as she came over to me in the living room.

"I'm assuming that's your piece of cake and mine is safely in the fridge," I said, eyeing her plate.

"You're cute," Mom said.

"Uh huh. So, what did you have to wear?"

"Oh, look at the time. I'm going to bed," she said, putting the plate of cake down on the table in front of me.

"Nobody took a picture of you?"

"Nope. Can you believe that?"

"You're holding that purse mighty tight there missy," I said, noticing her firm grip on her bag.

"Yes, well, I really love this purse," she said, patting it affectionately.

"You have pictures in there."

"You calling your mother a liar?" Mom accused.

"Yes, I am."

Mom gave in and handed it over. "Hmm, well, that's why I ate your cake."

I opened it up and pulled out a bunch of Polaroids. "Oh my God."

"Be nice," Mom warned.

"You look like Nancy Reagan," I said, giggling.

"Oh now, how is that nice?"

"I don't believe this. You look so completely different. Elegant, understated . . ."

"Yes, well, I was wearing underwear with propellers on them if it makes you feel better. I'm going to bed." Mom held out her hand for the pictures.

"I'll send the Secret Service up," I said as I put the photos back in the purse and handed it to my mom.

"Oh, by the way," Mom said, stopping on the landing, "I would put on your good pajamas, you know, the cute ones with the cakes on it, and brush your hair, and put on a little lip gloss."

"Why?" I asked.

"You're being kidnapped tonight," Mom said quickly and ran up the stairs.

"Excuse me?" I got up off the couch and followed her.

"I got a call today from Francie," Mom explained as we walked into her room.

"What?"

"Yes. She said that she and her friends were going to come in while you were sleeping, wake you up, kidnap you, and take you out to breakfast in your pajamas."

"Why would they do that?"

"Apparently it's fun."

"Well, that doesn't sound fun."

"She told me to leave the key under the mat and some money on the coffee table."

"And you said yes to this insanity?"

"Hey, I told you not to become a soche. But you didn't listen," Mom said as she emptied the contents of her purse.

"I can't believe you are going to let a group of strange girls come traipsing in here and take your only child, your precious baby girl, off to God knows where in the middle of the night."

"If it's someplace with doughnuts bring me one, okay?" Mom said, pulling the pictures out of her purse to put them away.

"Fine." I started to leave her room, then stopped, went back, and grabbed the photos out of her hands.

"Hey," she protested.

"Christmas cards," I said as I walked out of her room.

"More like your Grandmother every day!" Mom called out after me.

I changed into some cute pajamas, brushed my hair, and put on a tiny bit of lip gloss, then returned to the living room to continue my book. A little while later, I heard a car pull up outside the house. I closed my book, got up, and headed to my room. "Mom! My kidnappers are here!" I called upstairs.

"Okay. Have fun," Mom said, sleepily.

I got into bed and pretended to be asleep. A few minutes later, I heard a group of giggling girls open the kitchen door then sneak into my room.

"Get the light," Francie whispered.

"I can't find it," Ivy whispered back.

"Shh," warned Francie.

Then the lights came on and Francie, Ivy, and Lem, all dressed in normal clothes, and a couple of girls in pajamas, including Paris, stood around my bed. "Surprise," they all shouted.

"What's going on?" I asked groggily, as if woken from deep sleep.

"Rise and shine," Francie said brightly.

"You can grab shoes but no socks," Ivy instructed.

"Oh wow, this was totally unexpected. I'm completely surprised," I told them.

"You looked it," Francie said, pleased.

I got up to get my shoes.

"Okay, let's move," Ivy said. "We've still got a couple of more girls to get."

I put on my shoes as the girls walked out of my room. Paris stopped by the door, her hair a rat's nest pulled back by a large headband and her face dotted in zit cream. She was wearing a big, bulky Ebenezer Scrooge-y nightgown. "So, that's how you look when you've just woken up?" she said to me.

"Um . . . yeah," I lied.

"Nothing in my life is fair," Paris said under her breath as she turned and walked out. I followed.

We got into the cars and went off to get the other pledges. Once everyone was present, the Puffs blind-folded us and took us to our destination. They had us get out of the cars, still unable to see, and led us across a path to a door. The door opened and we filed into this unseen building and down a hallway.

"Okay. That's far enough," Francie said as she in-structed us to stop. "Ladies, here on this spot, tonight in this place where so many others have come before you, we invite you to join us."

"Ladies, remove your blindfolds," Ivy instructed.

We took off our blindfolds and looked around.

"We're at Chilton," I realized.

Francie turned to Ivy. "Keys, please."

"What are we doing at Chilton?" I asked.

"Will you please be quiet! We are being Puffed!" Paris said to me.

Ivy pulled out a set of keys and handed them to Francie.

"What you are about to do and what you are about to say will remain forever between the members of the Puffs and only the members of the Puffs," Francie stated sternly. Then she turned and opened the door. Everyone followed when she walked into the office. When I got up to the door, I noticed the nameplate and suddenly stopped, Paris and Lisa, another pledge, next to me.

"This is the headmaster's office!" I said, panicked. "How did she get the keys? I'm sure he didn't give them to her."

"Stop it!" Paris said, agitated. "We are making very important social contacts here."

"Hey, I'm not looking for social contacts," I replied. "I have friends. I'm fine."

"Well, how nice it must be to be you. Maybe someday I'll stumble into a Disney movie and suddenly be transported into your body and after living there a while I'll finally realize the beauty in myself. But until that moment I'm going to go in there and I'm going to become a Puff! Now get out of my way!" And Paris charged into Headmaster Charleston's office. Lisa looked at me sheepishly, then followed Paris. I sighed and walked in after them.

Francie arranged us in a circle, and Ivy lit a candle and brought it solemnly over to an ancient bell on the headmaster's desk. Then Francie started the ceremony. "The historical bell of Chilton. A hundred and twenty years old. Every member of the Puffs has stood here under the cover of night to pledge her lifelong devotion to us." She picked up the candle and placed her hand on top of the bell and very solemnly recited the oath of the Puffs:

*I pledge myself to the Puffs,*
*Loyal I'll always be.*
*A "p" to start, two "f's" at the end*
*and a "u" sitting in between.*

I glanced over at Paris, who was mouthing along. "Anne Sexton, right?" I muttered when Francie was through. Paris glared at me.

"Once you've finished your oath you will ring the bell three times," Francie instructed.

Ivy turned and told me I was first. I looked around at the extremely serious faces peering at me. For Harvard. I walked over to the bell and candle.

"Uh . . . 'I pledge myself to the Puffs . . . '" I started quickly and slightly embarrassed.

"You have to hold the candle," Ivy reminded me.

I picked up the candle and started again. "I pledge myself to the Puffs, loyal I'll always be . . ."

"Sing out, Louise," Francie said.

I continued louder but still as embarrassed. "A 'P' in front, two 'f's' on the end and a 'u' sitting in between." And then I hit the bell once. Then twice. I was just about to hit the bell a third time when a voice warned, "I wouldn't do that again, Miss Gilmore."

We all turned and looked quickly at the door. The lights went on and there stood Headmaster Charleston, security guards flanking him.

∽8

Headmaster Charleston had us sit in a line and asked Mrs. Traiger to call our parents, and then came the lecture.

"Disappointment? Disillusionment? Frustration? Astonishment?" he started, pacing back and forth in front of us. "I suppose you could say I am experiencing all of these emotions. Finding some of Chilton's best and brightest acting in such a destructive, immoral, and illegal manner will make all of us think long and hard about the manner in which we are educating you girls."

I shifted a little in my seat, angry that I was there.

"But that is all in the future," Headmaster Charleston continued. "How do we handle this now? Well, suspension will be considered. Detention and extra credit to maintain your current GPA standing will be a given."

"This is unbelievable," I muttered under my breath.

Bionic Man Charleston turned to me. "What was that, Miss Gilmore?" he asked sternly.

"Nothing," I replied.

"No. I distinctly heard you mumbling something in a rather disgruntled tone. I'd like to know what it was."

I got up from the couch and faced him. "I said this is unbelievable."

"And just why is this unbelievable, Miss Gilmore?"

"Because I didn't even want to be here in the first place."

"Oh now, Miss Gilmore . . ."

I interrupted him. "Things were going fine. My grades were good, I joined the paper, my routine was down—"

"Your routine was—" Headmaster Charleston started to interject.

"And I have friends," I continued, cutting him off. "I have a steady boyfriend, and my mother and I are freakishly linked, and Lane and I have been best friends since kindergarten. But you don't see that because I don't live in this town and if you don't see it, then it must not be true and you call me in here to lecture me because I'd rather read at lunch than endlessly discuss the euthanasia of homecoming."

"Your reading had—"

But I had more to say. "You told me and you told my mother that I needed to socialize and if I didn't it would be frowned upon and it would hurt me getting into Harvard."

"Well, yes, we did say that—"

"So I did it. I sit down at a table. A random table."

"Random!" Francie said, insulted.

"And the next thing I know, I'm being pulled out of my bed in the middle of the night and I'm blindfolded and then, before I know it I end up here with the Ya-Ya Sisterhood reciting poetry and lighting candles and now I'm going to be suspended? Because I was trying to do what you told me? What's fair about that?"

Mrs. Traiger came through the door and announced the arrival of the parents.

"Thank you, Mrs. Traiger." Headmaster Charleston turned back to us. "All right, ladies. We will continue this conversation tomorrow and for many days after that. You may go."

Everyone got up and headed for the door. "Miss Gilmore," Headmaster Charleston said, stopping me. I turned and looked at him. "I think that maybe you and I should talk some more," he said.

"About what?"

"About the fact that though I do feel it is important that students socialize, possibly we may have been a little hasty to judge in your case," he replied.

"Really? So does that mean that you might reconsider my suspension?" I asked.

"You're an excellent student. You deserve to go to Harvard. I wouldn't want to stand in the way of that. We'll talk tomorrow."

"Thank you." I turned and walked out of his office. When I got to the hallway, I found a group of parents chastising their kids. I looked over at Paris, who was being led away by a maid yelling at her in Portuguese.

My mom approached me, semifrantic. "What happened?" she asked, kissing me on the forehead. "The reception on the phone sucked and all I heard was 'Rory,' and 'Chilton,' and 'get down here.' Whose butt do I have to kick?"

"We didn't go to breakfast," I told her.

"What are you talking about?"

"We came here, they broke into the headmaster's office as the big initiation," I explained.

"Ugh, those stupid girls."

"Mm hmm," I said, nodding my head. "Part of the initiation was ringing a bell. So that's what I was doing when security showed up and they called you."

"That's what you got busted for, ringing a bell?"

"Yeah, uh huh."

"That's it? Bell ringing?"

"Yes," I repeated.

"Were you at least smoking a Cuban cigar while you were doing it?"

"Mom—"

"No. I mean, bad girl. How many times have I told you not to ring bells?"

"Let's go," I said.

"They can dent or scratch and they make dogs crazy. Who do you think you are, the Hunchback of Notre Dame? Are you French? Are you circular? I don't think so," Mom went on.

"I'm walking to the car now." I turned away from her and started down the hall.

"Wait, hold on," Mom said, stopping me. "How much trouble are you in? Should I go talk to the head-master?" she asked, concerned.

"No, I think things are going to be okay."

"Okay. Was it a big bell at least?" she asked as we walked off, her arm around me.

∽

The next schoolday at lunch, I entered the dining hall, my tray, backpack, book, and portable CD player in hand. I passed the Puffs and continued to my usual table, putting my tray down. I took off my backpack, then sat down and put on my headphones. "It's Alright Baby," by Komeda started up through the headphones when I hit the "play" button and I opened up my book and started to read. Then I realized that once again, someone was standing over me. When I looked up, I saw Lisa, one of the girls to be initiated at the ill-fated Puffs ceremony. I took off my headphones.

"Do you mind?" Lisa asked, indicating the empty spot across the table from me.

"Oh. No," I replied.

"Thanks." Lisa slid into the seat, putting her tray next to her. I put my headphones back on as she grabbed Mary McCarthy's *Memories of a Catholic Girlhood* off the tray and started to read. And together but separate, we had lunch.

## ❧9

I kept waiting for that phone call from Grandma about my near suspension but it never came, so I was a little nervous that Friday as we drove to my grandparents' house for dinner, not sure what to expect. Mom reassured me if Grandma had known, we would have heard about it by now. And she was right. My grandmother was in fine spirits when we arrived. My grandfather was out of town, so the three of us sat at the dining room table and started our dinner.

"How's the meal?" Grandma asked.

"Tasty," I replied.

"Very tasty," Mom agreed. "New cook?"

"Yes," Grandma said. "Marisela. She's introduced us to some wonderful dishes, so charmingly specific to her native country."

"What country is she from?" Mom wanted to know.

"One of those little ones next to Mexico," Grandma responded.

"How charmingly specific." Mom smiled.

"Too bad Grandpa's out of town. He likes weird food," I commented.

"Yeah, where's he eating his weird food tonight?" Mom asked. "Argentina? Morocco?"

Grandma hesitated slightly before answering. "Akron."

"Ohio?" I said.

"Yes," admitted Grandma.

"Get out of here," Mom said.

"I will not get out of here," Grandma replied strongly.

"No. I didn't mean really get out of here, I —"

"Why is Grandpa in Akron?" I interrupted.

"I don't know," Grandma said.

"It was just a saying," Mom said, trying to defend herself.

Grandma ignored her. "They sent him to deal with some problem with their local office down there."

"A saying," Mom went on. "You know, like 'save me' or 'get me out of here.' Things like that."

Grandma turned to Mom. "Lorelai, would you like me to put a mirror in front of you so you can look at yourself while you have this conversation?"

"Sorry. Dad's in Akron . . ."

"Yes. The amenities are atrociously lacking. He had to eat at a coffee shop last night. The whole thing's terribly insulting. He's miserable," Grandma told us.

"I hate that he's miserable," I said sincerely.

"So do I," Grandma replied. "We really ought to do something."

"Yes, I agree," I said.

"Warning, warning . . ." Mom said quietly to me.

"I'm glad to hear you say that, Rory," Grandma said, "because I thought of a wonderful way to cheer him up."

"Cool, what?" I asked Grandma.

"Danger, Will Robinson. Danger," Mom piped in. I glared at her.

"An oil portrait of you for his study," Grandma said grandly.

"An oil portrait?"

"I tried, have fun!" Mom said to me.

"It could hang right over his mantel. He'd just love it," Grandma went on excitedly.

"Oh. Well . . ." I hesitated.

"It would make him so happy," Grandma continued.

"Well, I guess that would be okay," I said.

"Oh, Mom, please, don't make her do this."

"She just said she would," Grandma replied looking at my mom.

"Fine. Paint the picture, but don't make her sit and pose for it. Paint it from a photo."

"A photo?" Grandma was appalled. "That's what they do at malls."

"I'll sit, it's fine."

"Just because your own experience sitting for a portrait was bad doesn't mean Rory's has to be," Grandma said.

I turned to my mom. "What portrait? I haven't seen this."

"They never finished," Mom stated proudly.

"Three painters started and they all three quit," Grandma told me.

"Why'd they quit?" I asked.

"She wouldn't stop scowling," Grandma answered, eyeing my mom.

"I was going for a Billy Idol thing," Mom said to me.

"The one from Italy had some sort of breakdown," Grandma continued.

"Oh my God," I said.

"Hey, it didn't hurt Van Gogh. The guy should thank me," Mom defended.

"A year later, I swear I saw him rummaging through our recyclables," Grandma went on.

"Well, I'm happy to sit," I said. "It's for Grandpa, so why not?"

Grandma was pleased. "Wonderful. I'll set it up first thing in the morning."

"Psst. If you want, I can teach you the Billy Idol," Mom whispered loudly to me.

"Most people focus on the lip thing, but the eyes are just as impor—" Grandma slammed down the salt shaker, cutting off Mom's statement. And we went back to the charmingly specific meal in front of us.

With my educational future safe for the moment, Mom had a renewed interest in getting the inn she and Sookie had always dreamed of. Her engagement and subsequent breakup had distracted her from it, but with that now behind her, she again focused on her original goal. They had already found the perfect spot, an old abandoned building formerly known as the Dragonfly Bed and Breakfast and Mom recently put in a title request to see who owned the dilapidated inn. It turned out that Fran from Weston's Bakery was the title holder, but when Sookie and Mom went to see if Fran would sell, she wouldn't. Seems the property's been in her family forever, and with her being the last Weston, she felt it was the only family she had left. That certainly wasn't the answer Mom and Sookie were looking for and when Mom got home from seeing Fran, she was really depressed. I had just started my breakfast and offered to come by the inn when I was through to help out, hoping that would cheer her up. She smiled at me and said that would be great, then went off to work.

I finished up, then headed out to the inn, running into Lane on the way. She was going home and hopefully straight to her room. If she got there after her mom's Bible study group started, she would be stuck downstairs for the duration of the meeting, and the last time that happened, three members of the group declared Lane perfect for their sons and she was trapped into going on three horrible blind dates. That would not happen again, she vowed. She continued filling me in on her life, telling me that Janie Fertman, one of the cheerleaders at Stars Hollow High, was trying to be her friend again. Lane was so *not* cheerleader material.

"Yikes," I said. "What kind of vibe are you giving her?"

"Oh, my patented Keith Richards circa 1969 'don't mess with me' vibe with a thousand-yard Asian stare thrown in there," she answered.

"That should do it," I told her. A siren went off and as we rounded the corner, we saw a crowd outside Doose's Market. A fire truck was already there as a police car pulled up. "What's happening up there?"

We crossed the street and made our way through the crowd. Police tape surrounded the store, and a chalk outline of a body, indicating someone had died there, was drawn into the asphalt in front of the entrance. A thoroughly agitated Taylor was talking to Officer Scanlon, one of Stars Hollow's police officers. She told him to hang tight and walked over to her partner for a moment. We got to the front of the crowd and found Dean.

"Hi," I said.

"Hey," he responded, moving aside so we could get a better look.

"What's going on?" I asked.

"I don't know. I got here and this is what I found. I mean, I told him it looked fake, but he didn't believe me," Dean said.

"And you have got such an honest face," I said, looking up at him.

"Well, he must not love me as much as you do," Dean replied, smiling at me.

"Okay, you two are officially sickening," Lane said as she turned around and made her way out of the crowd and to the safety of her room. Officer Scanlon headed back over to Taylor. "Everyone's accounted for, Taylor. Looks like this is just an elaborate prank," she told him.

"But it looks so real," Taylor replied. "Where'd they get the police tape?"

Officer Scanlon shrugged. "Kids have their ways."

"Who'd be depraved enough to pull a stupid prank like this?" an angry Taylor asked.

"Hard to say," answered the officer.

I looked away for a moment and saw Jess leaning against a lamppost across the street. He was watching the whole event with a rather amused look on his face. He caught me looking at him, then turned and walked away. I was fairly certain I knew who that depraved individual might be.

I continued on to the inn and found Mom and Sookie in the kitchen. I sat at Sookie's desk and Mom brought over some receipts that needed to be sorted. I flipped through them as Sookie prepped the next meal.

"Mom, you're not writing what you purchased on the back of any of the inn's credit card receipts," I said.

"Oh. Well, just put cooking spray and . . . sponges," she replied.

"Okay . . . and when an auditor asks why you purchased such large amounts of cooking spray and sponges?"

"Then I drop my pencil and I put the scoop-neck sweater that I am now making a mental note to wear to good use," she answered, walking over to me with a fresh cup of coffee.

"Well, as long as you have a solid, well-thought-out plan," I said, turning back to the receipts.

"I had a dream last night," Sookie said to my mom. "About us and Fran."

"Ohhh, what was it?" Mom asked.

"Well, it was the future, and we were all old. You and me and Rory and Jackson and Michel, everyone. Gray hair, walking around with canes and we were all kind of ailing, you know, had those big cataract glasses on, you were hard of hearing and kept going 'Huh? Huh?'"

"Oh, that's attractive," Mom said.

"It's you kids with your rock and roll," I remarked.

Sookie went on. "But what ho, here walks up Fran and guess what? She looks exactly the same. Even better."

"Oh, now that's not fair," Mom said.

"The woman's going to live forever," stated Sookie.

"Not necessarily," replied my mom. "Hey, did you look up angina? I forgot to."

"Yeah. It's nothing major." Sookie turned back to her chopping.

"You guys have got to stop talking like this," I said.

"Like what?" Mom asked.

"We love Fran, remember? Fran is great," I reminded them.

"No, honey, of course we love Fran," said Sookie, "we just want to know what God's ultimate plans are for her, that's all."

"It's such the perfect place," Mom said dreamily.

"It's perfect in every way," added Sookie.

Rory with her father, Christopher, at the Debutante Ball

Presenting . . . Lorelai Gilmore

Rory contemplating
the Fan Dance
✧

Lorelai and Emily
watch as Rory is
presented to society.
✧

*Richard and Rory at the Debutante Ball*

Rory, escorted by Dean

Rory with Debutante Ball cake

Luke's nephew, Jess

Paris during the Puffs initiation

Rory at a
Friday night dinner

Jess returning "Howl" to Rory

Headmaster Charleston reprimanding Rory
after the Puffs incident

Sookie, Lorelai, and "Juliet" Rory

"I don't even want to think about looking elsewhere," Mom continued.

"It's worth waiting for," Sookie went on.

"Totally worth waiting for," Mom agreed.

"I would advise at least pretending to look busy," Michel interrupted, entering the kitchen. "The boss is here."

I looked at my mom, excited. "Mia!"

"You're kidding?" my mom said, equally thrilled. "When?"

"I just spotted her walking in," Michel told us.

"Let's go!" And Mom and I rushed out to the lobby.

# ∽10

Mia owns the Independence Inn and gave Mom her first job when she left my grandparents' house shortly after I was born. Mia is like family, but she travels a lot, and a few years ago she moved to California, so we just don't see her as much as we used to or as much as we would like. She was talking to one of the inn employees when we got to the lobby. "Mia!" I called out. She broke off her conversation when she saw us. "My babies!" Mom and I ran over and we all embraced, almost knocking each other down.

"Did we know you were coming?" I asked.

"*I* didn't know I was coming," she answered.

"This isn't a surprise inspection, is it?" Mom said.

"That's exactly what this is. Ready?"

Mom and I stood straight, side by side, and Mia circled around, examining us. "You're too thin, as always."

"But we eat," I told her.

"And you're both too beautiful . . ." Mia continued.

"Yes. That's true," Mom replied. "We often feel guilty

monopolizing the amount of beauty we're in posses-
sion of."

"And I don't see you enough, which is my fault, so
you both pass," Mia finished, giving us both a huge hug
again. Michel wandered over to where we were standing and Mia went up to him. "Michel . . . oh, how nice
to see you. Oh, and look at that suit. You are quite the
dandy, aren't you?" Mia turned him around and Michel
smiled proudly.

"Well, I had a feeling that a lovely woman was going
to be visiting today so I decided I must look my best for
her," replied Michel in his heavy French accent.

Mia looked at him for a long beat. "I'm sorry, honey,
I didn't catch a word of that."

"He says he missed you," I interpreted.

"You've been in the U.S. quite a long time, Michel.
Your enunciation really should be better by now," Mia
said.

"The customers seem to understand me just fine," he
replied.

"I didn't get that either," Mia said, turning to us.
Then she went back to Michel. "Did you get the tapes I
sent you?"

"Hey," Mom said to Michel, "maybe you should hit
the desk, a couple of people are looking for help."

"Right away," he said to my mom. "Mia, I—" he
started, then thought better of it. He gave her a little
salute and walked away.

"So, are you too busy to sneak out with me for a
walk?" Mia asked.

"Not if it's okay with the boss," I said with a smile.

"It's a demand at this point," Mia said.

"Let's go." Mom turned to the front desk. "Hey,
Michel, hold down the fort?"

"It's a little slow now, so it's no problem," Michel replied.

Mia looked to me for help. "He said he's never liked you and that you're a problem," I translated.

Michel was horrified. "I said no such thing," he protested.

"I don't know where this hostility comes from," Mia said, playing along. "Can we work this out?"

"There is nothing to work out," Michel insisted.

"He told you to get out," I told Mia.

"I did not!" Michel insisted.

"I don't know what I did to make him hate me," Mia added for Michel's sake, as we all headed out the door.

As we passed Weston's Bakery, Fran was outside sweeping her sidewalk.

"Hello, Mia. Hello, girls," Fran called out as we passed.

"Frannie! Sweetheart! My God, you look wonderful!" Mia responded.

"I feel wonderful! Like a million bucks in fact," Fran said with a huge smile.

Mom looked a little disappointed when Fran said that, and when she looked over at me, she saw me staring at her, shaking my head in disapproval. "Evil," I whispered to her as Mia continued talking to Fran.

"I was thinking nothing," Mom defended.

"Evil and going to hell," I continued.

"Well, at least I look good in red," Mom replied.

Mia asked Fran to send the tasty black and white cookies to the inn and we continued on our walk.

"Oh God," Mia said, "I've missed this. I've missed this town and the people and—" She glanced at my mom. "You look guilty."

Mom denied it, so Mia turned to me. "What did she do?"

"I didn't do anything," Mom insisted.

Mia ignored her and continued pressing me. "Was it really bad?"

"I'm not saying anything," I told her.

"Oh my," Mia said, shaking her head.

Mia wanted to stop in at Luke's so we entered to find Luke at the counter tinkering with a broken toaster oven. Mia looked around the diner. "Look at this place. Exactly the same." Luke looked up and when he saw Mia, ran over to greet her.

"Actually, I made him paint a few months ago," Mom said proudly.

"Well, good for you," Mia said.

"Mia, hey," Luke said, giving her a huge hug.

"Nice to see you, Lucas," she replied affectionately.

"You're the only person in the world that can call me that, Mia," Luke told her.

"I know this," Mia answered.

"I'm saying it for others who plan to try it later," Luke said, eyeing my mom.

"Whatever, *Lucas*," Mom replied.

"Mia, you know anything about toasters?" Luke asked.

"Not a damn thing," she answered.

"Well, then sit down and let me get you some coffee." Luke went behind the counter and put on a fresh pot of coffee as we sat at a table.

"So, talk to me, you two," Mia said. "Tell me everything. How are your parents, Lorelai?"

"My parents are . . . my parents," Mom answered, resigned.

"They're good," I answered for my mom.

"They're good at being what they are," Mom clarified.

"Which is lovely people who sometimes forget to show it . . ."

"In the way that sharks hunting for chum forget to show it," Mom added. "So, how's living in Santa Barbara?"

"Horrible," Mia answered. "Did you know the damn sun shines all the time out there?"

"They've written songs about that," I told her.

"Well, no one told me that's how it was. Half my wardrobe is obsolete," Mia said.

"Oh. Drag," Mom said. "Hey, you know, the vintage-y blue coat—"

"You're not getting it," Mia stated.

"Right," Mom said.

Luke had gone back to the toaster oven while waiting for the coffee when Jess came out from the back of the diner and watched him struggle with the appliance. "You're making that worse," he said to Luke.

"Big help, thanks."

"Luke's nephew," Mom informed Mia.

"Luke, that's your nephew?" Mia asked.

"It's Liz's kid," he explained, coming over with the coffee and mugs, Jess following. "Jess, this is Mia. She owns the Independence Inn."

"Huh," replied Jess.

"That's 'Hello, nice to meet you' in Slacker," Luke told Mia.

"You don't need me down here, do you," Jess said as he turned around and headed upstairs.

Luke apologized for Jess, and Mia was understanding. "You weren't exactly a talkative boy yourself when you were his age," she said to him.

"That's right, you knew Luke as a boy," Mom said, brightening.

"I can't imagine Luke as a boy," I said to Mia.

"Well, he was much the same as that young man. Very curt, didn't suffer fools gladly, or nonfools for that matter. Kept to himself . . ." Mia told us.

"Can we change the subject?" Luke asked.

"He would help people carry groceries home—" Mia continued.

"Wow, how very Boy Scout-y of you," I said.

"—for a quarter a bag," Mia added.

"Wow, how very John Birch Society-y of you," Mom said.

"He was never without his skateboard for a time—"

"Were you any good?" Mom asked.

"I could hold my own," Luke answered.

"Then there was that year you wore that same shirt everywhere you went."

"I don't remember that," Luke said nervously.

"Must've been something flannel," Mom said.

"No, it was from that TV show, that . . . famous one."

"It's not important," Luke said quickly.

"*Star Trek*, that's it."

Mom and I burst out laughing. "Oh my God! Oh my God!" Mom taunted.

"Stop it," Luke said.

"You were a Trekkie?" I asked, unable to wipe the huge smile off my face.

"I was not a Trekkie."

"Oh-oh. I do believe that denying that you were a Trekkie is a violation of the Prime Directive," Mom stated.

"Indubitably, Captain," I affirmed.

"It was a gift from my aunt. I wore it to make her happy," Luke said.

"I never wanted to make any aunt of mine that happy," Mom said.

"Did I say something I shouldn't have?" Mia asked.

"No, no, Mia, I'm just going to have to cancel everything I have scheduled for the next three months 'cause I'll still be laughing my ass off," Mom said.

The bells on the door clanged and Taylor entered, loaded for bear. "Luke, I need to talk to you, right now," he said.

"What is it, Taylor?"

"I have conducted a thorough investigation of all the people who may have inadvertently been witnesses to the phony murder at my store last night."

"There was a phony murder?" Mia whispered to us.

"Yeah, this town's too dull to work up a real murder," Mom replied.

"But you're one 'Beam me up, Scotty' reference away from being the victim of one," I said to Mom.

Luke walked away from Taylor and busied himself behind the counter.

"Luke, are you going to listen?" Taylor demanded.

"What's this got to do with me?"

"Three people have reported seeing Jess in that area late last night. Skulking. Lurking."

"There were a lot of people out late last night. I know, because I fed some of them. I'll give you their names and you can add them to your suspect list," Luke responded.

"Another person witnessed Jess walking out of an arts and crafts store two days ago with what appeared to be chalk," Taylor continued.

"You *appear* to be bugging me, Taylor."

"What are you going to do about it, Luke?"

"About what?"

"About the results of my investigation?"

"Absolutely nothing. But thanks for the info."

"You have to do something. People want action."

"People. Meaning you," Luke clarified.

"It's not just me," Taylor stated. "I speak for the Stars Hollow Business Association, the Stars Hollow Tourist Board, the Stars Hollow Neighborhood Watch Organization, and the Stars Hollow Citizens for a Clean Stars Hollow Council."

"All of which are you," Luke said.

Taylor was getting angry again. "So are you going to act?" he wanted to know.

"Yes, I am," Luke replied. "I'm gonna act like you never came in here."

"Fine. Have it your own way. But I warn you—there's gonna be a lot of unhappy people at the S.H.B.A., the S.H.T.B., the S.H.N.W.O., and the S.H.C.C.S.H.C."

"F.I.N.E." Luke retorted.

"Ah, you are impossible! You are impossible!" Taylor shouted as he headed out. Then, warm and sweet, "Oh hi, Mia."

"Nice to see you, Taylor," Mia acknowledged.

Taylor stormed out and Luke resumed his work behind the counter.

"Oh, I've got to get out of Santa Barbara," Mia remarked. "I miss the small town theater." Then, looking at us, she added "And I miss you. Hey, do you realize that it was fifteen years ago, almost to the day?"

Mom smiled at her. "Yes, it was."

"What was?" I asked.

"To the day when this skinny little teenage girl showed up at the inn," Mia replied. "How did you find us?" she asked Mom.

"Star of Bethlehem . . . and the Yellow Pages," Mom answered.

"She had this tiny little thing in her arms . . ." Mia remembered.

"A little thing named Rory," Mom said, pinching my cheek.

"Okay, no physical reenactments," I said.

"You marched up to me, looked me right in the eye, and said, 'I'm here for a job. Any job.'"

"Well, IBM had turned me down for the CEO slot, so I was desperate."

"Work experience? None. Recommendations? None. Skills?"

"Besides flawlessly applying mascara in a moving car, none," Mom answered for her.

"Not one thing to recommend hiring her. Just that, mm, how do I put this and remain a lady . . . that 'who cares' look in her eyes. So I gave her 'any job.' The other maids hated you."

"Yeah, well, they were so slow," Mom said.

"You were special," Mia said affectionately.

"Mia, why don't you move back here? We miss you," I said.

"Or at least visit more," Mom added. "You never check in. You used to come all the time."

"I don't have to. You've made me redundant," Mia said to Mom.

"I have not," Mom protested.

"Don't be humble. The inn is beyond covered. It's never run this well, or been this successful," Mia said. Mom and I glanced at each other, then we looked down at the table, feeling rather guilty. "That inn is like your place now," Mia continued, not noticing our reactions. "Without you, I wouldn't know what to do, I'd be lost."

"Lost, yeah . . ." Mom said.

"Yeah . . ." I added.

"You look sad now. Why?" Mia asked.

"Oh, nothing," Mom said quickly, taking a sip from her coffee mug. I looked up and tried to smile reassuringly at Mia.

∽

I went to Grandma's the next day for my portrait sitting. She was thrilled when I arrived and quickly put me in a gown, took me out to the patio, and sat me in a large chair. The portrait painter was set up and ready to go. Grandma asked me to raise one arm. It was unbelievably uncomfortable and I kept shifting, which annoyed the painter. Finally, Grandma got so frustrated she called Mom to tell her how impossible her child was being.

"She won't pose in an appropriate manner," Grandma said into the phone.

"I'm trying to, Grandma, it's just awkward," I called out. I wasn't doing it on purpose, but sitting still with an arm over my head was really hard. Plus, Grandma had wanted a swan in the portrait and the swan really made me nervous. They're mean. In fact, the swan was running around the patio right now and the handler was trying to corral it in and not having much success, as he didn't want to get too close either. If I weren't in the middle of all the action, I might have found the whole thing rather amusing.

"I suppose you'd just have her sitting in a chair reading a book," Grandma said into the phone.

I perked up. That sounded great. Mom must have agreed because Grandma's reaction was less than enthusiastic. But Mom must have persuaded Grandma it was a good idea because she had me put my arm down and told the handler to take the swan away. I let out a sigh of relief as I lowered my arm, and the swan let out a scary, enormous wail. In protest? Or relief?

Then Grandma and I went into their library and chose an appropriate book for the portrait — Walt Whitman's *Leaves of Grass*. Ah, much better, I thought, as I settled in with the book and the painter started his work.

☙

There was a town meeting that night so Mom and I stopped at the inn to pick up Mia and together we headed over to Miss Patty's.

"We're late," I said anxiously to my mom. I hate being late.

"We're not late," Mom replied.

"The last time we were late Taylor said there would be consequences," I reminded Mom.

"He did not. He said there would be severe consequences," Mom corrected.

"Mia, what time is it? Are we late?" I asked.

"I hope so," Mia replied.

"Mia!" my mom chastised.

"I'm sorry, but it's been two years since I've gotten to go to a town meeting and I want some controversy."

Luke had just come out of his diner and was locking up as we passed. "Aha!" Mom said, startling Luke.

"Jeez. Don't sneak up on me like that," Luke said.

"Yeah, boy I was lucky you had your phasers on stun, huh?" Mom quipped.

I giggled. "Well, at least we're not late," I said. "Luke is never late."

"Actually, we're two minutes early," Luke informed us.

"Yeah!" Mom said.

"We should get a prize for being on time," I added.

"Hey Luke, let's go back to the diner and get pie for us as our reward for being on time," Mom said.

"Then you'd be late," Luke answered sensibly.

"A funny conundrum," Mom said, "but I want pie!"

"You're harassing me now," Luke said.

"I'm not harassing you. We're your groupies," Mom said. Then, like a bobby soxer, she continued, "Oh, Luke, you're so dreamy. Be my guy."

"No, be my guy," I said.

"I'm bringing up the need for more police protection at this thing," Luke replied dryly as we walked up the stairs to Miss Patty's studio.

We opened the door and walked in and were surprised to find the place full, the meeting clearly in progress. Taylor was at the podium, Miss Patty seated next to him. Everyone turned around and looked at us rather guiltily when they saw us enter. Mia turned gleefully to my mom. "I think we're late."

Luke demanded to know what was going on. "The meeting was supposed to start at eight, Taylor," he said, looking at his watch. "It's a minute to eight."

Taylor finally admitted they had started the meeting early to deal with a special issue pertinent to the business community.

"I'm in the business community, and I wasn't told about it," Luke argued.

Everyone in the room shifted around and looked at each other uncomfortably. Then Taylor admitted Luke wasn't invited because they were discussing the Jess situation.

"The Jess situation?" Luke asked, boiling mad. He turned away from Taylor to regain his composure. Mom and I hustled past him to grab some seats in the back row, Mia going the other way to get the seat on the end.

"Uh oh," I said.

"If this was the Wild West, we'd be pushin' the horses aside and divin' into the water trough right about now," Mom whispered as we slid into our seats.

"Damn it, Taylor!" Luke yelled.

"Luke, honey, calm down," Miss Patty said.

"After all," Taylor continued, "this is all your doing. If you hadn't so cavalierly dismissed the issue, we wouldn't have had to do this. I lost business because of what your hooligan nephew did."

"How was business lost, Taylor?" Luke asked. "If you opened a little late that day, your customers just came back later."

"Not so. When Mrs. Lanahan couldn't buy her head of lettuce that morning for her lunch, she drove straight to Woodbury to buy lettuce from a competing market," Taylor stated. "Isn't that right, Mrs. Lanahan."

Seated in front of us was the very old Mrs. Lanahan, who was very asleep. Taylor prompted her awake before continuing. "Word has it that she was telling other Doose's Market shoppers that the Woodbury lettuce is crisper. That's business flying out the door."

"Okay. Fine," Luke said, charging to the front of the room, pulling his wallet out of his back pocket. "How much is a head of lettuce, Taylor? A buck?" He slammed a bill on the podium. "Give me five heads."

"This goes well beyond a head of lettuce, young man. The charges against your nephew are numerous. He stole the Save the Bridge money."

"He gave that back . . ." Luke replied.

"He stole a gnome from Babette's garden."

"Pierpont was also returned."

"He hooted one of my dance classes," Miss Patty added.

"He took a garden hose from my yard," Fran piped in.

"My son said he set off the fire alarms at school last week." said Andrew, another townie.

"I heard that he controls the weather and wrote the screenplay to *Glitter*!" Mom threw in for good measure.

Then Bootsy stood up. Since it was apparently Attack Luke Day at the town meeting, he started bringing up issues with Luke that went back to when they were in the first grade. Taylor interrupted the bickering boys and brought it back to the present. "Boys, please. The bottom line here is that there is a consensus amongst townspeople who are in agreement that Stars Hollow was a better place before Jess got here."

"So this half of the room gets the tar, and the other half gets the feathers?" Luke said, frustrated. He stormed to the back of the room.

"Well, there's been no talk about tar and feathers," Taylor said, "Although—"

"Look, I've lived in this town my entire life. Longer than most everybody here," Luke started.

Bootsy interrupted. "Beg to differ. I'm five weeks older than you, that means I've been here five weeks longer."

Luke ignored him and continued. "I've never bothered anyone, I've kept to myself, and I've done the best I could. I pay my taxes and I help people when I can. I haven't pitched in on the decorative pageantry town stuff, because it all seems insane to me, but I don't get in the way of that stuff either."

"What's your point, Luke?" Taylor asked.

Mom stood up. "His point is—" She turned to Luke. "Do you mind?"

"Be my guest," he replied.

Mom continued. "His point is that if there's a problem—"

"And I'm not saying there's a problem—" Luke interrupted.

"Right, he's not saying there is a problem—then give him time to deal with it before you storm his diner with torches and pitchforks," Mom completed.

"Right," agreed Luke. "What I'm dealing with, being a problem that I don't necessarily agree that I even have." Mom looked at him, not really sure what he just said. "Right," she agreed anyway.

"I didn't get that last part," Taylor said, confused.

Mom simplified it for him. "Lay off him, because what you're all doing stinks."

"I'm done here," Luke said. "I'm done with all of you. Oh, and I was going to stay open late in case anyone wanted to eat after the meeting. Forget that." And Luke walked out of the meeting, people complaining about the loss of a postmeeting treat. "His turkey burgers are very dry," I heard Bootsy claim as we walked out the door.

"Well, I must say that was quite exciting," Mia said as we walked down the steps outside Miss Patty's.

"And a little disturbing," Mom added. "I think the whole town needs a field trip."

"You think Luke's okay?" I asked.

"I think he will be," Mom said. "He just needs to cool off a little."

I felt really bad—Luke was doing a great thing helping his sister out, and the town was turning on him. And Jess wasn't making things easier for him, which also pissed me off. Add to that the fact that my boyfriend had been scraping the outline off the ground for the last two days. I decided I would go check on Dean.

"Good idea. There's nothing like your face on his to make the cleaning process go faster," Mom said.

"She's all yours, Mia," I said.

"I'll take her," Mia answered, wrapping her arm around Mom's shoulder as they continued walking down the street.

Mom was asleep by the time I got home and a little crabby the next morning when I left for school. She was still at work when I got home from school, but Dean came by and we went off to Luke's to get some coffee.

"Hey, I've gotta drop by the market," he said as we walked the street.

"But it's your day off."

"Yeah, it's to get my paycheck. If I don't get it by four, Taylor locks it in a safe and it's on some kind of timer and then when I complain, he lectures me about promptly putting checks into the bank and the theories of compound interest and my head hurts from all the nodding I do even though I don't listen and—"

"Go, go," I told him.

"I'll just be a minute." And he disappeared inside the market as I waited outside. After a minute, Jess walked up to me.

"Should you be standing here all alone? I hear this is a pretty dangerous corner."

I was still a little miffed from the town meeting. "I'm fine," I replied curtly.

"Feeling succinct today?" he asked.

"Pretty much."

"Hmm." He paused a moment. "Did I do something to offend?"

"Me?"

"Yeah."

"Nope."

"Good."

"You might ask that same question to Luke, though," I told him.

"Meaning?"

"You've got the whole town down on him."

"Really? How'd I do that?"

"You know how you did that."

"Well, I'm not familiar with the bluebook laws in this town, so you could be talking about a lot of things. Dropping a gum wrapper. Strolling arm in arm with a member of the opposite sex on a Sunday—"

I pointed to the ground where the chalk outline could still be faintly seen.

"Ah . . ." said Jess. "What about it?"

"You did it. The whole town knows you did it. They had a meeting about it."

"So you actually went to that bizarro town meeting? Those things are so *To Kill a Mockingbird*."

"Yes. I went. And Luke went. And when he got there everyone ganged up on him. They all want you gone."

"Wow. Bummer."

"And he's standing there yelling at everyone and defending *you* and paying Taylor back for his lettuce losses—"

"His what?"

"And now Luke's a pariah, and it's all because of you."

Jess didn't respond.

"What a shock. You don't care about any of this," I said, angry.

"I didn't say that."

"Go. I'm tired of talking to you," I said, waving him off.

"Fine." He turned and walked away.

"You care nothing of Luke and his feelings!" I yelled, stopping Jess.

"Got a second wind, huh?" he said, turning around, heading back to me.

"All he does is stick up for you and all you do is make his life harder. I guess that's what you have to do when you're trying to be Holden Caufield but I think it stinks. Luke has done a lot for my mom and a lot for me and I don't like him attacked. Okay, second wind over." I turned away from him. Jess stood there for a minute.

"I didn't know they were coming down so hard on him," he finally said.

"Funny I never pegged you as clueless. My mistake."

"Okay. I get it."

I turned and looked at him.

"I do," he insisted. "I get it."

I kind of believed him.

"So did you at least think it was funny?" Jess asked.

I tried not to, but I couldn't help but smile a little at the memory of the outline. I stifled the smile. "That is so not the point," I told him.

Jess smiled. "Yeah, yeah, you thought it was funny," he said, smiling.

"I got it," Dean said, coming out of the store. He noticed Jess. "Oh. Hey."

"Uh, Dean, I don't think you guys have met. This is Jess," I introduced. To Jess, I said, "This is Dean."

"Boyfriend?" Jess asked.

"Of course," I answered.

"Sorry, you didn't say," he said to me. "How you doing?" he asked Dean.

"Good. Good," Dean answered.

"Okay," I said quickly, "so, see you 'round."

"Seems to turn out that way, doesn't it?" Jess replied as he walked off. We turned and continued on to Luke's.

∽

That night, Mom and I were at the front door of Grandma and Grandpa's house. Mom was still in a bad mood.

"I wonder if Grandpa is still in Akron," I asked as she rang the doorbell.

"Well, for Akron's sake, I hope he's moved on to Boise," she answered.

Yet another new maid answered the door. "Hi, we're the daughter and the granddaughter," Mom said abruptly as she barged past the maid. I smiled apologetically and followed my mom.

"You are majorly crabby," I said as we entered the house.

"I just have a headache," she replied.

Grandma came up to greet us. "Oh good, come, come, come, it's all done and it's great," she said excitedly as she led us into Grandpa's study and presented the portrait to us.

"Ta-da," Grandma said proudly.

"Whoa . . ." I said.

"What do you think?" Grandma asked.

"It's . . . freaky," I replied.

"Freaky?"

"Well, just seeing me . . . here . . . up on the wall like that, it's, uh . . . I like it, though. It's good. I guess. It's just . . . I should probably take myself out of the judging process."

"I think Richard's just gonna love it, it's the perfect thing, don't you think?" Grandma asked Mom.

"Mm hmm," Mom said brusquely.

"You've got to admit," Grandma said proudly, "it turned out better than you thought it would."

"Yeah," Mom said, still curt.

"Well, come on. Say a little more than that," Grandma encouraged.

"It's great, Mom. It's fabulous. It's just a notch below Rembrandt," Mom answered sarcastically.

"Well, you don't have to take that attitude," Grandma said.

"What do you want from me? I'd light some sparklers and jump up and down yelling, 'Yay for the painting' but I'm fresh out of sparklers and my feet hurt too much to jump. But I promise next week when I have more energy I'll write a love song for the chandelier."

Hurt by that outburst, Grandma walked out of the room. "Mom . . ." I gestured toward the exiting Grandma. Mom turned and followed Grandma into the kitchen. They both emerged a few minutes later and everything seemed fine, but dinner was unusually quiet that night.

After we left, I made Mom tell me why she was so crabby. After the town meeting, Mom had told Mia about her plans to start an inn with Sookie. Mia was amazing and supportive and asked Mom if she could do it sooner rather than later as she had been looking for a reason to sell the inn. Mom had such a severe emotional reaction to the thought of the inn, the place she considered home, being sold that she started to doubt her abilities to start a place of her own. She took it out on Sookie, criticizing everything she did, and they wound up in a huge fight. That was earlier that day. She couldn't get her mind off it. She knew she was wrong, but didn't know how to make it up to Sookie, to tell her she did have faith in her and believed they could have a successful inn together. She was depressed about the whole thing and unsure of how to approach Sookie.

The next day Luke came over to weatherproof the chuppah he had originally built for Mom and Max's wedding. He mentioned Sookie had stopped by the diner and quickly changed the subject when he asked how their plans for the inn were going so he gathered maybe things weren't going so well. Mom spilled everything to him, how she freaked out when Mia said she would sell the inn and how she took that out on Sookie.

Luke reassured her she was just scared just like everyone else is when they take on something big. He told
her about his first day opening the diner. He was so nervous he ran to the back, threw up, banged his head on
the floor, and passed out. It took about a year for him to
start having fun. So what she's feeling is normal.

So Mom went to the inn and apologized to Sookie
and told her she still wanted to start the inn with her.
Sookie was understandably cautious, and made Mom
promise she wouldn't flip out like that again because
she couldn't take losing her business partner and best
friend in one swoop. Mom agreed, and now their inn
plans are back on track.

"Oh, man, it's such a relief to have that Sookie thing
fixed," Mom said as she related the end of the story to
me while we were having breakfast at Luke's.

"I know. I hate fighting with friends," I replied.

"That's what enemies are for."

"And God knows we have our share of those."

"People who eat crunchy food with their mouths
open."

"People who dog-ear library books."

"People who spit when they talk."

I rubbed my face. "Oh, gross, you got me in the eye."

"I did not."

"You totally did."

"You're full of it."

"Luke, where's my toast?" I asked.

"It's gonna take a while," he replied. "My big
toaster's broken, so I got stuck with just this dinky one."

Jess turned around, hit the button on the big toaster
and popped it back, then he turned around and continued wiping off the counter.

"How'd that happen?" Luke asked, surprised. He hit

the button and popped it back up again. Again, it worked perfectly.

"You're gonna break that," Jess said to Luke.

"It was broken before," Luke said.

"Well, it must've got better," Jess stated.

"Inanimate objects don't usually get better," Luke replied. "Did you fix this?"

"Please," Jess said dismissively.

"Jess . . ."

"I have no idea what you're babbling about. I don't fix things."

"But yesterday it—"

"I got school." Jess headed for the door, grabbing his coat on the way. As he opened the door, he shot a glance at me. I smiled approvingly and he exited. Maybe he wasn't such a bad guy after all.

# ❧ 11

Selfishly, I was really glad Mom and Sookie had made up. In addition to her just being really sweet, she was also an incredible cook, Mom's other best friend, and, well, at times, it helped to have her around. This evening, for instance, Sookie and I were in the kitchen staring at a large box. She had come over and we decided to watch a movie so Mom ran to the video store to pick up a couple of options. While she was gone, this box was delivered, addressed to Mom and Max, obviously sent by someone who hadn't heard the wedding was off. We were *dying* to know what was in the box, so we placed it on the kitchen table and waited for Mom to get home, positioning ourselves in front of it so the box wasn't the first thing she saw when she walked in.

"I'm back!" Mom called out from the front door a few minutes later.

"Kitchen," I called back.

"Okay, now I couldn't make up my mind so I got *The Shining* and *Bringing up Baby*," she said as she headed toward us. "Now, I know you're thinking one's a movie about a homicidal parent. And the other one's—" She entered the kitchen and stopped when she saw us standing there, presumably looking guilty. "Hello," she said warily.

"Hi," said Sookie.

"Hi, Mom."

"What'd you break?" Mom asked.

"Nothing. Well, the broiler, but this came for you," Sookie told her.

We moved aside, revealing the large wrapped gift on the table.

"And Max," added Sookie.

Mom walked over to the box. "We're thinking it's a wedding present," I said.

Mom read the address label. "'Lorelai Gilmore and Max Medina.' Wow, guess news doesn't always travel fast."

"Are you going to open it?" Sookie asked.

"Nope," Mom replied.

"But—aren't you curious?" Sookie wanted to know.

"Just leave it there, I'll return it tomorrow," Mom said.

"But there's no return address," I told her.

"Is there a card?"

"Nope," Sookie said.

"Maybe there's one inside," I said hopefully.

"With the return address on it," Sookie added.

"'Course that means you'd have to open it to find out," I completed.

"Fine, give me a knife," Mom said. I ran to grab one.

"Oh, it's so exciting . . ." Sookie said. My mom shot her a look. "Maybe not."

I handed her a knife, then after she ripped through a

piece of wrapping paper, helped her tear the rest of it off the gift, exposing a large chrome machine. "An ice cream maker!" I said excitedly.

"A Musso Lussino 4080!" Leave it to Sookie to know the make and model.

"Someone sent me a fascist ice cream maker?" Mom wanted to know.

"Italian design, stainless steel body with a chrome finish," Sookie said reverently. "I didn't know these were even available in the States."

"And no card," Mom said. "Perfect."

"It has its own freezing unit so you don't have to prechill." Mom tried to interrupt but Sookie was too excited at this point. "And Jackson just got his apple crop in. We can make cider ice cream!"

"Yes, we can, using his ice cream maker, but Il Duce here is going back," Mom said firmly.

"To where? Maybe it's an orphan," I told her.

"That's right. We'd be giving it a home," Sookie added.

"Okay, once again, I bring up the fact that this is a wedding present, and as I am not getting married, neither God's law nor Emily Post's allows me to keep this," Mom said emphatically.

"But isn't there a rule about late presents?" I asked.

"Like if they arrive after a certain date, the giver forfeits all rights of return?" Sookie added.

"Exactly," I punctuated.

"Nice try," Mom said.

"It's true," Sookie went on. "I saw it on Martha Stewart. She was doing one of those double programs. And the first half was on massaging your dog, she had this chow, and she was rubbing it—"

"Sookie—" Mom interrupted.

"But the second half was about gifts, and she said if it arrives more than ten weeks—"

"Eight," I corrected.

"Eight weeks then you don't have to return it."

Sookie and I crossed our arms, rather pleased with our argument.

"Okay," Mom said, "clearly, this is shaping up to be one of those moments that St. Peter is going to show on a big video screen when I die, and I for one do not want to see the three of us staggering around with cider ice cream slathered all over our faces while my soul hangs in the balance. So, until I find out who sent this, no one goes near it. And," she added, picking up a videotape, "we're watching *The Shining*."

She turned and walked into the living room. Sookie and I looked sadly at the ice cream maker.

"I bet Max would've let us keep it," Sookie said solemnly as we followed my mom to the other room for our movie.

∽

Things had been relatively normal at school since the Puffs incident. Paris and I had even quietly worked out a system where she didn't hate me while we worked on the paper together. So I should have known that peace wouldn't last, right? Yeah, I know. But I didn't. I was in Professor Andresen's Shakespeare class, taking notes as she lectured.

"Believe it or not, Shakespeare probably never intended his plays to be read by students sitting at desks, more concerned with getting A's than with the fate of Macbeth. His plays were meant to be experienced, lived. So, with that in mind . . ." She started passing out papers. "Together with my third-period Shakespeare, you'll be split into five groups, and each group will assume responsibility for one act of *Romeo and Juliet* which will be performed a week from Sunday. You will nominate a director, you will cast the scene, rehearse the scene, and interpret the scene in your own individual manner. Last year we did *Richard III*. One group did their scene as the Mafiosi, another set it during the Roman Empire, and my favorite was the climactic last scene set during the last days of *The Sonny and Cher Show*. Just remember, whatever interpretation you choose should highlight the themes you see in the scene." The bell rang and everyone started to get up. "And if the love of the Bard's language still doesn't inspire you, remember, this will be fifty percent of your final grade," Professor Andresen added.

The class emptied out and I sat there a moment with Paris, Madeline, and Louise. We all looked at our papers.

"Act five," Madeline said cheerfully.

"Act five," an indifferent Louise stated.

"Act five?" Paris asked me.

"Act five," I answered, resigned.

Paris sighed. "Why don't they just sew our sides together and rename us Chang and Eng."

We got up and headed out of the classroom. Henry approached me as I entered the hallway.

Henry Cho is this Korean-American boy with a great smile who met Lane at Madeline's party last year. He zeroed in on her the second she walked through the door, and though she hesitated at first, she now thinks he's totally and completely perfect boyfriend material. But there's the Mrs. Kim Factor. And in her very Lane logic, she is convinced if she tells her mom she's dating a

Korean boy she would approve of, things could only go downhill. So Henry calls me, I get Lane on the phone, and that's how they talk. It's my duty as best friend. Besides, I like Henry. And it's amusing to see Lane gush about a Korean boy, the very thing she's been avoiding her entire life.

Henry held up his paper. "Act three. Swordfight. You?"

"Act five. Death scene."

"Nice. So, tonight, eight o'clock?"

"I'll tell Lane."

Paris came up and very sweetly said, "Rory, sorry to interrupt, hi Henry, but see, we're all standing over there trying to map out a game plan and a rehearsal schedule, and I'm sure whatever the two of you are talking about over here is so much more fascinating and important and well, gosh, let's just say it, fun. But I'd like to get an A on this assignment and in order to do that I'm afraid you're going to have to discuss your sock hops and your clambakes some other time. Okay? Thanks." She smiled at us and walked away.

"Well, that was scary," Henry said.

"It's going to get scarier when she gets a megaphone in her hands," I told him.

Henry walked away and I headed over to Paris, Madeline, and Louise. "So, I say we meet in the cafeteria," Paris was saying. "The acoustics are very similar to the Grand Hall and . . . oh, well, look who showed up."

"Sorry."

"Save it," replied Paris.

"Well, well, well, look who's back from suspension," Louise said, looking past us down the hall.

We all turned to see Tristin with Duncan and Bowman, two older boys.

Tristin Dugray was the biggest mistake I ever made. He had been nothing but mean to me since I had started Chilton, always calling me "Mary" (as in Virgin), but when Dean and I broke up for a short while last year, I ended up kissing him at Madeline's party. It was awkward at first, but Tristin and I talked about the kiss and agreed it had happened only because of our recent breakups. It was the first time he seemed like a normal person to me, and I felt so comfortable after that that I convinced him asking Paris out on a date would be a good idea. He said he would think about it and did end up taking her out. Paris was over the moon. But Tristin really wasn't that interested, and when she found out the only reason Tristin had asked her out was because I suggested it, she despised me even more than she had before the date. Like I needed to give her another reason to hate me. I hadn't really seen much of Tristin since then. Once school had started up again this fall, he'd been suspended more than he'd actually been in class.

"Tristin got suspended again?" I asked.

"Oh, like you hadn't noticed he'd been gone," Paris said snidely.

"What did he do?"

"He took apart Mr. Macafee's car and put it back together in the science building hallway," Madeline told me.

"You're kidding," I said.

"Well, he didn't do it by himself. Duncan and Bowman were there too," Louise explained.

"Plus the mechanics that they paid to do the actual work," Madeline added.

"Hey, anyone stupid enough to hang out with Butch Cassidy and the Sundunce Kid deserves whatever they get," Paris stated.

"When did he fall in with those guys?" I asked.

"The new year started and there they were. All three of them, side by side," Madeline said.

"Practically dressing the same," Louise said.

"It's very *On the Town*," said Madeline.

Paris walked off and Madeline and Louise followed. I glanced back at Tristin, then turned back and followed them down the hallway.

When I got home that night, Mom was in the living room, on the phone, pen and list in hand, making good on her promise to find out who had sent the wedding gift. I had stopped at Luke's on the way home and bought her some coffee. Mom nodded gratefully at me as I handed her the cup, then I went to my room to hang up my school jacket. I walked back out to the living room and sat next to her on the couch as she hung up the phone, sighing in frustration.

"How scary is it that my parents are turning out to be the normal ones in the family?" she said.

"No luck?"

"Well, I've still got the Pennsylvania Gilmores . . . How was your day?" she asked as she put down her list.

"I have to perform act five of *Romeo and Juliet* with Paris, Madeline, and Louise," I told her.

"Really."

"Paris has appointed herself as director."

"Nice. What part are you playing?"

"I'm not sure yet. She's still mulling over the screen tests right now and we're gonna find out tomorrow."

"Screen test."

"Twenty-four takes."

"I so want a copy."

"Forget it."

"I'll sell it on the Internet. Make a fortune," she said, getting up from the couch and heading for the kitchen. Like a commercial announcer, she continued, "First we brought you Pamela and Tommy Lee. Now prepare yourself for the crazy antics of Rory and the Bard."

I picked up the list she left behind and flipped through it. "Oh, and I told Paris that you would make all of our costumes so she wants to have a concept meeting with you tomorrow at three."

"What?" Mom said as she reappeared in the doorway holding a container of Cool Whip and a spoon.

"Yep. She needs a resume, and samples of your previous work, and referrals . . ."

"And my bare butt to kiss?" Mom said through a mouthful of Cool Whip.

"If you think that'll help set you apart from the other applicants, yes. Hey," I said, referring to the list, "I didn't know there was someone in our family named Bunny."

"Oh," Mom replied solemnly, "cross her off the list."

"Poor Bunny . . ." The phone started to ring, and I reached over to pick it up. "Hello?"

"Hey," said Henry.

"Henry, hi."

"Am I late?" he asked.

"No, right on time. Hold on." I pushed a button on the phone.

"Hey hon," Mom interrupted, gathering her things together, "I'm heading for class. There's pizza slash Luke's money on the table for dinner."

"Thank you," I said as I punched in the speed dial button for Lane's house and Mom went back to the kitchen to get more of her stuff. Mrs. Kim answered the phone.

"Hello, Mrs. Kim, this is Rory. May I please speak with Lane?" I said into the phone.

"Lane is studying," Mrs. Kim said curtly.

"Mama? Is that for me?" I heard Lane call out in the background.

"Why?" Mrs. Kim demanded to know.

"Well, I was just expecting a call from Rory and—"

"You do your math?" Mrs. Kim inquired.

"Yes."

"History?"

"Yes."

"Biology?"

"No."

"Why?"

"I'm not taking biology."

"Why?"

"I took it last year."

"And that's it? One year and you know all there is to know?"

"Well, I—"

"Tomorrow we look into private school."

"Mama, please, the phone."

"Five minutes. I'm counting."

"Hello?" Lane said into the phone.

"Lane, hold on." I pushed a button and patched Henry in. "Henry?"

"Here," he replied.

"Lane?"

"Here," she answered.

"Okay, you guys. Talk to you later." I smiled and hung up the phone, giving them their privacy. I picked up Mom's list again.

Mom walked into the living room with her jacket on, book bag in hand. "Okay. I'm gone. Hey, do me a favor and make some of these calls for me?"

"Don't you think you may be going a little bit far with this?"

"What do you mean?"

"I mean, I understand that you want to return the ice cream maker, but you did make an honest effort to get in touch with the person who sent this to you, and —"

"It's called closure, hon. I need it. Okay?"

"Okay." I took the list, all business. "Uncle Randolph . . ." I picked up the phone as Mom walked out the door. "Oh, sorry, guys," I said into the phone as Mom turned back. "They'll be off in a sec," I told her.

"Okay, but don't wait too long. I think Randolph was Bunny's older brother."

"Got it."

And Mom left for class while I waited for Lane and Henry to finish their conversation.

∞

Our Shakespeare group met after school the next day in the cafeteria. I walked in to find Louise filing her nails and Madeline flipping through a copy of *Jane* magazine. A somewhat nebbishy-looking boy was also sitting there looking completely uncomfortable and out of place. I crossed over to the table.

"Hey."

"Hey," replied Madeline.

"We're the Monkees," sang Louise, completing the phrase.

"Where's Paris?" I asked, sitting down.

"She'll be here in a minute," Madeline replied. She said she had to get some things."

I looked at the boy next to me. "Hi, I'm Rory,"

"I'm Brad. I'm from the third-period Shakespeare."

"He's the answer to our lack of boys problem," Louise informed. "Isn't that swell?"

"Well, maybe we should start," I suggested.

Madeline looked up from her magazine, surprised. "Without Paris?"

"That could be lethal," Louise said, still filing her nails.

"We could at least talk about what motif we want to do," I said.

"We're doing traditional Elizabethan," Paris stated as she walked in carrying a large box of props.

"Elizabethan?" I said as Paris put the box down. "But I thought the point of this was to—"

"The point is to get an A," Paris interrupted, "not to make *Romeo and Juliet* into a Vegas lounge act. Besides, we have the death scene. It's classic. It's famous." Then noticing the new guy, she asked, "Who are you?"

Brad was almost shaking as he answered. "I'm, uh, Brad. I'm from the third-period Shakespeare. Ma'am."

"Okay," Paris said as she handed out a photocopied booklet, "now I want everyone to read the chapters on acting I've photocopied out of Houseman's memoirs tonight. Everyone will be off book by Friday, and if you plan on missing a rehearsal you'd better bring a coroner's note." She pulled a sword out of the box.

"Tell me you didn't just have those lying around," I said.

Paris ignored me and turned her attention to Brad. "We're short on boys. That makes you Romeo." Brad was horrified. Paris continued. "Louise, you can play the Friar."

"Excuse me?" Louise protested.

"Well, well. The gang's all here," Tristin interrupted as he entered the room. He came over to the table, flipped a chair around, and sat down.

"This is a meeting," Paris informed him.

"Yeah, sorry I'm late."

"What do you think you're doing?" Paris said.

"Professor Andresen forgot to include me when she made up the groups," Tristin explained, "so she told me to pick one."

"Fine, you have four other acts to choose from. Take your pick."

"Yeah, well, Summer's in act one. Beth and Jessica are in act two. Kate's in act three. And Clare, Kathy, and Mary are act four, so this is the only one free of ex-girlfriends," Tristin said.

"So we're being punished for our good taste?" Paris asked sardonically.

"Oh, Paris, you hurt me. Do you no longer have any need for me at all?"

"Yes, we have great need," Louise said, sitting forward. "You can be our Romeo."

"Brad is Romeo," I said quickly.

"Put in your other contact, Grandma. Tristin is Romeo. Brad can be the second guard on the left," Louise went on.

"No," Paris said emphatically.

Madeline looked up from her magazine. "But she's kind of right, Paris. Tristin was born to be Romeo."

"Hey, I'm the director and I'll decide who's born to be what and Brad is Romeo," Paris insisted.

"Hell hath no fury like a woman scorned," Louise said, not too quietly to Madeline.

"What'd you say?" Paris asked.

"Just perhaps that someone is letting her personal feelings interfere with her leadership?" Louise said directly to Paris.

"My only feeling is that I don't want to give the most important part to someone who can't even manage to stay in school," Paris argued back.

"I'm just going to say one thing." Louise paused for a moment. "Fifty percent of our final grade."

Paris stood there fuming, torn.

"Is there going to be any scratching involved or is this just a verbal thing?" Tristin asked, thoroughly enjoying the trouble he'd caused.

Paris turned to me. "What do you think about this?"

All eyes turned to me. "Well . . ." I looked at Brad. "How are you at speaking in front of a lot of people?"

"I tend to throw up," Brad quickly answered.

I looked at Paris. She sighed and directed her attention on Tristin. "Fine! But I swear, you flake on this, and you'll pray you get suspended."

Tristin's pager went off. He checked it, then said he had to run. "Are we done here?" he asked as he got up.

"Rehearsal, tomorrow night," Paris called as Tristin walked out the door.

"Good," Louise said, pleased with the outcome. "So now Brad can be Friar Tuck, and I can be Juliet."

"Wrong," Paris replied.

"Hey," protested Louise.

"Juliet is supposed to be chaste."

"Oh." Louise returned to her nails.

Madeline sat forward. "Then—" she said hopefully.

"And she has more than three lines," Paris told her.

"Oh." Madeline sat back and returned to her magazine.

Paris turned to me.

"Oh no," I protested.

"Oh yes," Paris replied.

"No."

"Too late," Paris informed.

"How is it too late? We haven't done anything yet."

"You're Juliet. You're the best public speaker here, you've definitely got that waif thing down, and you'll look great dead. Next order of business. I did some location scouting this morning and I think the courtyard out back . . ."

Paris continued talking but I stopped listening. I couldn't believe I had to play Juliet to Tristin's Romeo.

I met Mom after school for some coffee and then we walked home. She was excited because she had decided to accept her first post-Max date and would be going out with a guy from her business class who had been flirting with her for the last few weeks. It appears Mom would constantly take the last burrito from the vending machine and that somehow led to him asking her out on a date. I know, it's crazy, but I was encouraging and really happy that she was getting out.

We got home and Mom sat down at the kitchen table to do a little more work on my costume before her date. I got out of my school clothes and as I was heading back into the kitchen, Lane called. Her mother had originally said no, but was now letting Lane come to the play on Sunday. "That's amazing! What changed her mind?" I asked as I wandered into the living room.

"I let her watch the *Romeo and Juliet* movie with Leo and Claire Danes," Lane said.

"Really? I would've thought she'd hate it."

"Oh, she did. But trust my mom to turn one of the world's great love stories into a cautionary tale of what happens when children disobey their parents."

"So, I'm guessing you're not any closer to actually telling your parents about Henry," I said as I sat down in the living room.

Lane lowered her voice. "I mean, what are the options if I tell them? They hate him, and it's over. They love him, and he therefore becomes odious to me, it's over. Things are working fine the way they are."

"You mean calling him Rory on the phone in case your mom is listening."

"I've grown fond of my cage, Rory." Then Mrs. Kim called out for Lane so she said a quick goodbye and hung up.

Mom came in wearing Juliet's elaborate headdress. She turned around, modeling it for me. "What dost my lady think?"

"That you're going to be late for the joust?"

"I meant of thy lovely headdress crafted by thy mother's artful hand." She did a small little bow.

"It pleaseth me much, but hath my beauteous mother looketh at the time?" I pointed to the clock on the wall behind her.

She turned around. "Oh crap!" She pulled off the headdress and ran upstairs to get ready for her date as the phone again rang. I picked it up. "Hello?" It was Paris calling on her cell phone from Chilton.

"Two other groups are rehearsing at school in the Grand Hall even though I specifically reserved it for us way in advance and confirmed the reservation twice but whatever. They're going to be there and I don't want them spying on us," she said.

"I don't think the ending of Romeo and Juliet is exactly a secret."

"Hello, our interpretation."

"Oh. Right."

"I went on the Web and found a site called Miss-Patty.net. It's in your town."

"There's a MissPatty.net?" I said, surprised.

"Have you heard of it?"

"Well . . ."

"Is it big enough?" Paris interrupted. "The site says it's 720 square feet."

"You know, I'd just rather rehearse somewhere else."

"Look, I've got enough to worry about without you being embarrassed of where you live."

"I'm not embarrassed. I just . . . want to keep my school life separate from my home life. You know?"

"Tough. Madeline and Louise are already on their way. I'll see you in half an hour." Paris hung up.

I put the phone down and started toward my mom's room to tell her what had just happened when she came down the stairs, scanning the room. "Have you seen my bag with the beads and the fur, looks kind of like Stalin's head? Aha," she said as she found it.

"We're rehearsing here now," I blurted out.

"What?" Mom said as she went to the desk and rummaged through her bag.

"Our Shakespeare group," I explained, following her. "Paris didn't want people spying on us so now we're rehearsing in Stars Hollow. This sucks." I couldn't believe it.

"Well, now at least you don't have to drive to Hartford. What's with the face?" she asked as she turned around to the mirror on the wall, applying her lipstick.

"It's just . . . Tristin is in our group."

"Oh yeah, you told me."

"Right, so Tristin . . . he's in our group . . . so that means he's in, well . . . and Dean lives here . . . so this sucks."

Mom turned around and faced me. "Okay, you know what, Vanna, I'm going to need a few more vowels here."

"I have to tell him."

"Tell who?"

"Dean."

"Tell Dean what?"

"That . . . Tristin . . . and I . . . that we . . . kissed at that stupid party," I finally let it blurt.

"Oohhh," Mom said, a little surprised.

"I have no choice."

"Well . . ." Mom said as she started powdering her nose.

"Because if Tristin sees Dean, then he'll tell him, and then it'll be even worse because it'll be like I was keeping it from him."

"Okay, let's just calm down."

"Which I was. I was keeping it from him! I can't believe this! I have to tell him."

Mom thought about it for a moment. "You're right."

"I am?" surprised that she agreed with me.

"Uh huh. I think you should tell him," Mom said supportively.

"Of course, right, I have to."

"Yeah. Then, at the play, right as Tristin enters to find you dead and pulls out the vial of poison to kill himself, Dean can leap from the audience and rip his head off, adding a level of reality few productions have ever seen before. You'll get an A, the Actors Studio will go nuts, you'll have James Lipton asking you what your favorite swearword is. It's a great plan."

"You. Not helping," I said as I turned and went to the couch.

"To prevent a homicide, yes, I am."

I fell back on the couch and stretched out across it. "I've got to tell him. I don't have a choice."

"Okay, fine," Mom said, walking over to me. "Try it out on me first."

"What?" I asked as Mom lifted my legs and sat on the couch.

"Pretend I'm Dean. If you're going to tell him this, you'd better have down what you're going to say."

"Seriously?"

"Seriously."

I sat up, then took a second to gather myself. "Okay." I looked across the couch at my mom. "Dean," I said.

"Rory," Mom answered in a lower "Dean" voice.

I shot her a look.

"Sorry. Serious now."

I got myself together again, then began. "Okay. Dean. Remember last year when we had broken up . . . and we weren't together anymore because . . . we were broken up . . ."

"That's good. Mention it three times. Keep going," Mom said.

"And there was this party and I went. And, um, Tristin was there and somehow, I'm not really sure exactly how, but we ended up in this room together and we . . . kissed."

"You and Tristin?" Mom/Dean clarified.

"Uh huh."

"On the hand?"

"No."

"Cheek?"

"No."

"He kissed you or you kissed him?"

"Kind of . . . both," I answered.

"So you kissed him?"

"Yes."

"When?"

"I already told you three times, when we were broken up," I said, getting agitated.

"Okay, not a good idea to yell at him right now."

"Sorry."

Mom/Dean continued. "When during the breakup?"

"What do you mean?"

"I mean how long after we broke up did you kiss Tristin?"

"Um . . . just . . . the night after we broke up."

"You mean the night after I told you I loved you."

"Yes."

"So, the next night after I told you that I loved you, you kissed Tristin?" Mom/Dean asked.

"I'm a terrible person!" I realized.

"Hold on . . ." Mom tried comforting.

"He's absolutely right! He told me he loved me and the next night I go and I kiss Tristin."

"Hey, that was me, not Dean."

"I hate myself!"

"You didn't do anything wrong! You were hurt and confused and broken up. You did nothing wrong."

"Tell that to Dean."

"No, because we're not telling Dean anything."

"Mom . . ."

"Listen to me. I know you are Miss Honesty, I have seen the banner in the closet, but this is the kind of honesty that will only make you feel less guilty and it's going to hurt Dean very much. It's possibly going to screw up the really good thing you guys have going now. Do you want that?"

"No, I don't."

"All right then. Relax. Be calm. Everything will be fine."

She was right. "Okay."

"I gotta go. Can I ask you one more question?"

I looked up at her and nodded.

She lowered her voice and became Dean again. "Do you think my hair looks cool?"

"Bye," I said.

" 'Cause some days I look at it and I think, cool, and

some days, I think, could be cooler," Mom/Dean continued.

I pushed her off the couch as I lay back down. "I won't wait up for you."

"Like today I thought, left side cool, right side, not so cool," Mom/Dean went on as she got up from the couch.

I couldn't help but smile. "Bye," I said again.

"Bye," replied Mom as she grabbed her purse and walked out the front door.

I got to Miss Patty's Dance Studio and found Paris glaring at Miss Patty and her senior yoga class. Madeline, Louise, and Brad came in behind me.

"What's with the cast from *Cocoon*?" Louise asked.

Paris looked at the group. "Where's Tristin?" she asked. "He said he was coming with you."

"Oh, he's here. He just went over to the market," Madeline said.

I whipped my head around. "What?"

"He needed cigarettes. Just in case we didn't already know that he was bad," Louise told us.

"Um . . . I'll be right back," I said.

"Where are you going?" Paris wanted to know.

"I'll just be a sec," I said as I headed down the steps.

I raced over to the market and got there just in time to see Tristin drop some money on top of a broken bag of flour he had obviously just purposely dropped. Dean looked like he was ready to punch Tristin when I ran up and pulled him outside.

"All right! I'm outside," Dean said angrily.

"I'm really sorry I didn't tell you this before, but . . . Tristin . . ."

"—is playing Romeo to your Juliet. Yeah. I heard."

"But he wasn't even in our group at first and then no one else wanted him and then Paris moved our rehearsal spot to here and she did it today and I didn't have time to tell you."

"You and Tristin wind up thrown together a lot at that school."

"It's just a project. That's it. Nothing more."

"You and Tristin playing Romeo and Juliet. Perfect. Really, really amazing."

"I know you hate it."

"Oh yeah. I hate it. I really hate it.

"But we do the scene on Sunday and then it's over. And then it's back to 'Tristin? Who? I'm sorry, I don't know a Tristin.'"

"You must mean that young boy that got mysteriously strangled by a Doose's Market apron one night," Dean added.

"I heard about that. Awful. They say drugs were involved."

Dean halfway smiled at me.

"Please don't be mad. I'm sorry. I'm really, really sorry."

"Sorry about what? You didn't choose to do this with him, right?"

"No, I didn't."

"So then what do you have to be sorry for?"

I looked at him a beat. I couldn't tell him what I was really sorry for. "That . . ." I started, "that I didn't tell you about rehearsal. And that No Doubt is touring with U2. I know you're extremely disappointed in Bono."

Dean smiled at that. "All right, so when's this thing over?"

"Sunday," I told him.

"Okay." He leaned over and gave me a kiss. "I'm go-

ing to walk around the block, just . . . get him out of the
market."

"Right away," I said. Dean walked off and I watched
him for a moment, feeling a little guilty. Then I headed
back into the market to get Tristin.

After rehearsal, I went to Luke's for dinner. I was at
a table reading Alex de Tocqueville's *Democracy in America*, a burger and chili fries in front of me, when my
mom came in, still dressed up from her date.

"Oh, thank God, you ordered. I'm starving," Mom
said as she sat down next to me.

"What are you doing here? You were supposed to go
out to dinner."

"I did go out to dinner," she said, grabbing one of my
fries.

"Then why are you eating mine?"

"Well, he took me to this darling little place called
Minnie's. Very hip. Very chic. Very small portions."

"So, how did it go?"

"Well . . ."

"Ah."

"You know, we talked about all the things we had in
common and then the salad came."

"Not a soul mate?"

"He's never seen *Ab Fab*."

"Definitely not a soul mate," I said, digging my fork
into my chili fries. Mom continued telling me about
their differences, but said she was really glad she went.

"Yeah?" I asked.

"Yeah," she said with a smile. "I mean it was fun to
kind of get dressed up and have a freshly laundered
man open the door for me, and the best part about it
was it was no big deal. We laughed a little, we hugged
good night, I'll never date him again but I do believe the

burrito bit will live on. It was a totally casual date. I am now officially a casual dater."

"That's great. And we can celebrate by getting you your own plate of fries." Mom snuck a couple more fries off my plate as I turned around to call Luke. "Hey, Luke, can we get another round!"

"Coming right up," he called back.

"So, tell me about the big rehearsal," Mom asked as she grabbed my soda to wash down the fries.

"We got off to a shaky start, and Louise acts like she's the priest in a Madonna video, but by the end, we were not half bad."

"Good. Good," Mom said, smiling at me.

"Dean ran into Tristin."

"Oh. Bad. Bad."

"It's okay, though, because I pulled them apart without any bloodshed and I explained it all to Dean—"

"You explained it all to Dean?" she said, nodding her head encouragingly.

"I told him that Tristin wasn't supposed to be in our group and that Paris moved the rehearsal to Miss Patty's at the last minute and that's why he didn't know about it."

"Oh. That version of 'all.'"

"But Dean's fine now."

"He's fine?"

"He's fine."

Luke came over with a plate of chili fries and set them in front of Mom. "You want a burger too?"

"No, I'll just have half of hers," Mom replied.

"One burger, please," I requested.

"You look all dressed up," Luke commented.

"Do I? 'Cause I feel very casual," Mom answered. She smiled at me and I laughed a little. Luke shook his head, very used to us not making sense to him, and went to get Mom's burger.

The bell on the door rang and Dean walked in. "Hey," he said as he came to our table.

"Hi. You just get off work?" I asked.

"Yep," he answered.

"Hey, Dean. You want some fries?" Mom asked.

"No," he replied. "I'm actually going home for dinner. My mom made fried chicken tonight and she saved me some."

Mom was impressed. "Ooh, you've got one of those cooking moms."

"That's so nice," I added.

"Well, she may make chicken but is she a casual dater?" Mom smiled proudly.

"I hope not. She's married," I told her.

"Do I want to know what either one of you is talking about?" Dean asked.

"Nope," Luke answered as he went to the table behind us.

"My mother casually dated tonight," I explained.

"Well, congratulations," Dean said.

"Thank you. Thank you very much," Mom said, pleased with herself.

"I just wanted to know what time your rehearsal is tomorrow?" Dean continued.

"Five. Why?" I asked.

"Well, it's my night off and I thought maybe I'd come by and watch," he said.

"Watch what?"

"Watch you."

"Watch me do what?"

"Rehearse."

"Oh." I turned and looked at my mom. "Dean, I think you'd be really bored watching rehearsal."

"Yeah," Mom piped in. "I've dozed off twice just listening to her talk about rehearsal."

"I won't be bored," Dean insisted.

"But we don't even know our lines yet. You should just come on Sunday."

"That's a good idea. After all, Sunday is the day of rest. And that's what you'll be doing. Resting. 'Cause it's bo-ring," Mom said.

"Mom . . ."

"Well, honey, it's not your fault. You didn't write the damn thing."

"Well, I'll come on Sunday, too," Dean said.

"Okay, but if you're gonna go on Sunday you don't want to spoil it for yourself," I tried reasoning.

"What? Like I don't know how it ends?"

"Okay, Dean, look . . ."

"Rory, come on. I'll sit in the back, you'll die, and I'll walk you home. It's no big deal, right?"

"Right."

"Good. So, I'll see you tomorrow."

"Yep," I said as Dean got up from the table. "You sure will."

Dean leaned down to kiss me, then said goodbye to my mom and walked out the door. Mom looked at me. "Oh yeah. He's fine."

I sighed and went back to my burger.

∽

I decided my only option was to try and talk to Tristin so I went up to him the next day at school. He was leaning against his locker talking to Bowman and Duncan when I approached. "Excuse me, Tristin? Can I talk to you for a second?" I asked.

Tristin turned to the other boys. "I'll meet you guys

later, okay?" Duncan and Bowman took off, and Tristin turned back to me. "I'm all yours."

"I need to talk to you about something serious."

"Serious. Huh. I'm intrigued," Tristin said as he opened his locker and took out a couple of books.

"Dean's coming to rehearsal tonight," I told him.

"Wow. Are you sure they can spare him? I mean, what if there's a run on baked beans?"

"Will you just shut up for five seconds? Please?"

Tristin put up his hands, motioning he wouldn't say anything.

"Thank you. Look, as I said, Dean is coming to rehearsal tonight and I would like you to promise me that you won't say anything to him about what happened."

"What happened . . . ?"

"At the party."

"At the party . . ."

"Tristin! You and me at Madeline's party?" Tristin scratched his head in seeming confusion. "You had just been kicked to the curb by Summer and I found you sulking on a piano bench and I sat down, we talked, and then . . . we kissed!"

Tristin eyed me a moment. "That was you?"

"What?"

"Were you a blond back then 'cause—"

"You know what, forget it." I walked away. Tristin came after me. "Hey, Rory," he said, tapping my arm. I stopped and turned to face him, frustrated. "There is no point in talking to you," I said. "I knew that, yet I tried. Won't happen again."

"You don't want me to tell Dean that we kissed," Tristin said sincerely.

"By George, I think he's got it."

"Okay," he said, "if that's what you want."

"It is," I replied.

"Although . . . he's going to find out anyway," Tristin said.

"What?"

"Well come on, you know when we kiss on stage it's gonna be pretty obvious it's not the first time. I'm a good actor, but I can't hide that kind of passion."

"Look, things are going really good for me and Dean right now and I don't want anything to mess that up. Especially not something that meant nothing at all to me and I wish had never happened in the first place!"

Tristin looked at me a moment. "So, things are going good for you two, huh?"

"Yeah, they are."

"Good," he said brightly. "That's good." And he turned and started back toward his locker. I suddenly realized what I said might have hurt him so I followed. "So . . . what do you think?" I asked as Tristin opened his locker and put his books back in. "You just took those out," I pointed out as he shut the door.

"Well, I changed my mind," he said abruptly.

"Are you all right?" I asked.

"Yeah, I think somehow I'll recover from the news of the great romance between you and the Beav."

"A lot of stuff's been going on with you lately, huh?" I said.

"Meaning?"

"Just, you know, the car thing, the suspension thing . . . a lot of drama."

"Well, I get bored easily."

"Just doesn't really seem like you."

"And you know me now, huh?"

"I know that you don't get suspended for stupid pranks."

"I pulled stuff like that before I knew Duncan and Bowman, all right?"

"Well, if you did, you didn't get caught."

Tristin looked away, not answering.

"You're getting caught a lot," I continued.

"Your point being . . ."

"Maybe Duncan and Bowman aren't the best people to be hanging out with. They're not as smart as you, Tristin. They don't have as much going for them as you do. They—"

"You know, I'm going to have to bail before we get to the hugging part." And he walked off as the bell rang signaling the start of class. "And ask your boyfriend to remind me when it's coupon day, okay?" he called back to me. I watched him go, dispirited, then headed to my class.

I tried to take my mind off the situation but I couldn't. The rehearsal was quickly approaching and I was dreading it. I met Mom at Luke's but when our burgers arrived, I just wasn't hungry so mine sat on the plate at the counter.

"Taking pity on your burger?" Mom asked.

"Not hungry," I told her.

"Honey, you've got to eat. You're going to kill yourself in a couple of hours. You need your strength."

"Ha ha."

"Maybe Dean won't even come tonight," Mom said, trying to cheer me up.

"Oh, he'll be there. There aren't enough monster truck rallies in the world to keep him away from Miss Patty's tonight."

The diner door jingled opened and a young guy wearing a baseball hat, a South Park T-shirt under a jacket, and jeans came in with an older man and woman. They walked over to the counter next to us.

"Okay, that's it," Mom said. "This afternoon we are

going to engage in some intensive retail therapy to bring you out of this funk."

"No, thanks."

"I mean it. Today is the day we finally spring for the Powerpuff Girls shot glasses."

"I can't. I promised Lane I'd help her pick out an outfit for the play tomorrow."

"Lorelai?" the guy at the counter said to Mom. She turned to see who was addressing her. "Yeah?"

"Hey, it is you," he said. He turned to the older couple with him and said, "This is Lorelai. She's the girl I told you about."

"Oh, Paul!" Mom said, finally realizing who it was. "I'm sorry, I didn't recognize you with the hat."

"Yeah." Paul smiled broadly.

"What're you doing here?" Mom asked.

"I'm getting some coffee," Paul replied.

"In Stars Hollow?"

"Well, you know, you talked so much about the town the other night, and especially Luke's place, so . . . my mom's crazy for coffee, I thought I'd bring them up here for breakfast."

"The other night?" I asked quietly.

"Yes," Mom said, turning back to me. "Paul is my friend from the other night, the casual Wednesday."

"Ohhhh," I responded as I realized this had been Mom's date. Oh my God, he looked like he was twelve.

Mom introduced me to Paul, and he introduced us to his parents. "You ordering?" Luke interrupted impatiently.

"Luke . . ." Paul said. "Are you Luke?" He turned to my mom. "Is this Luke?"

"Yes. That's Luke," Mom confirmed.

"Oh man! Mom, Dad, that's Luke!"

"We have heard so much about you," Paul's mom said.

"Darn shame about that Rachel," Paul's dad added.

"Who the hell are these people?" Luke asked my mom.

"Uh, Paul is my friend. From business school," Mom explained.

"Yeah, we went out the other night and she talked about a few people in this town, you being one of them, so, nice to meet ya," Paul said excitedly.

"Yeah," Luke said gruffly.

"Um, okay, three coffees to go then."

Luke went to get their coffees, and I looked at my mom, grinning.

"Something funny?" she asked.

"Nope," I responded.

"You're just smiling for no reason."

"I'm a happy person."

Paul turned back to us, coffees in hand. "Hey, I've gotta run. My mom wants to go antiquing. So, it was nice meeting you. I'll see you in class, Lorelai."

Everyone said goodbye, and Paul left with his parents. Mom turned back to me. "What?"

"Nothing," I replied, trying desperately not to laugh.

"Say it."

"I've always wanted a little brother," I blurted out, giggling.

"He looked older the other night," Mom said defensively.

"How much older could he possibly have looked?"

"A lot. He's usually a little scruffy, and the baseball cap hides the funky hair thing."

"He should've been holding a yo-yo and a lollipop and wearing a beanie with a propeller on it."

"He's in his twenties."

"He must've been a very good boy to deserve a happy day like today," I said, still giggling. "I bet they let him ride a pony."

"Okay, aren't you supposed to be helping Lane?"

I got off the stool and kissed my mom on the cheek. "Thanks for cheering me up." I was suddenly starving so I grabbed my burger and walked out of the diner eating it.

Dean showed up as predicted and leaned against the wall to watch the rehearsal. I was lying on a table, seemingly dead, while Tristin stood beside me holding a vial of poison. Paris was in front of us, and Madeline, Louise, and Brad sat off to the side, watching.

"Here's to my love," Tristin as Romeo said. He downed the contents of the vial. "O true apothecary! Thy drugs are quick." He paused a moment over me, then stopped rehearsal by asking for his line. " 'Thus with a kiss I die!' " Paris said impatiently. "How hard is that to remember?"

" 'Thus with a kiss I die.' Right. And then I kiss her, right?"

"Yes! You say 'Thus with a kiss I die,' then you kiss her and die!" Paris said.

Tristin looked behind Paris and gave Dean a small superior smile.

"Why are you smiling?" Paris asked. "You think this is a joke? The performance is tomorrow!"

"Wait, tomorrow!" Tristin said with mock surprise. "Oh my God, I totally missed that the first forty-seven times you said it!"

"I warned you, I am not going to fail this because of you. I will replace you with Brad in a second."

"Oh dear God, no," Brad said nervously.

"Can we just get through the scene?" I asked, still horizontal.

"Please," seconded Madeline.

"Fine," Paris said. "But yell 'line' once more and you're out." She turned to Brad. "Start memorizing!" Brad quickly picked up the scene and started his work.

We began again. "O true apothecary! Thy drugs are quick! Thus with a kiss, I die." Tristin/Romeo leaned down to kiss me, then, glancing at Dean, pulled back before completing the task.

"What?" Paris demanded.

"It's just, with this being our last kiss and all, it makes me think of our first kiss. You know, at the party," Tristin mused.

I sat up. "What!"

"Lie down!" Paris directed, "You're dead!"

"We all are," muttered Louise.

Tristin turned to me. "You remember the kiss . . . in act one, at the Capulets' masked party?"

"What about it?" Paris asked impatiently.

"Well, I was just trying to think of something that would make this kiss as special as that one."

"Tristin—" I warned.

"I thought she could cry," Tristin said.

"What?" I said, horrified.

"She's dead! You're dead! Lie down!" Paris ordered.

"But that's the beauty of it. No one would expect her to cry," Tristin explained.

"I would," Dean interjected.

"You know, funny you should say that," Tristin said, pointing at Dean.

I stood up quickly. "I need to take five."

"You know what? Let's all take five. That way, you can all cancel whatever plans you had tonight because we're going to stay here till we get this right!" Paris stormed out of Miss Patty's. Madeline followed. Louise pulled out her cell phone and started to dial, then noticed as Brad pulled his phone out and flipped it open. "Who could *you* possibly be calling?" she asked as she walked past him and out the door.

I walked over to Dean and Tristin moved off to the side, pretending to study his lines.

"He is unbelievable," Dean said angrily.

"Dean, I really need you to leave," I said.

"What?"

"The play's tomorrow and it's fifty percent of my grade, and you standing there staring at Tristin, it's like a challenge or something."

"Well I don't like the way he's messing with you."

"I don't like it either but we have to get through the scene and we can't get through the scene with you standing there, so . . . Dean, please?"

Dean sighed, frustrated. "Fine. Call me later."

He leaned down to kiss me, glaring at Tristin behind me, then walked out the door.

"You know, I noticed you didn't cry when you kissed him," Tristin said, walking around in front of me. "I'm starting to feel insecure."

I turned on him. "What is wrong with you?" I said, furious.

"Whoa! I think I liked you better comatose."

"I thought you weren't going to say anything!"

"Did I say that?"

"You make it impossible for anyone to be nice to you! No wonder you had to join our group! Anyone who's actually suffered through the experience of going out with you would absolutely know better!"

Tristin's pager went off. He glanced at it, then said "Gee, I really wish I could continue your analysis of how pathetic I am. Unfortunately I have to meet some friends." Tristin grabbed his jacket and walked out just as Paris came back in to the studio behind me.

"Where're you going? Where's he going?" she asked, storming past me to try and get him back. "We're not finished! Hey! I'm the director here! Tristin!"

Brad followed Paris. "Tristin," he called out. "Come back! Please!"

I stood there staring out the door. How did this happen?

# ∽12

Mom, Sookie, Lane, and Dean stood in the back of a crowd of Chilton parents and students watching the balcony scene from act two, performed by a Caveman Romeo and Cavewoman Juliet. I ran up to them in my full Juliet regalia, elaborate headdress and all.

"Oh, look at you, you look just like a princess," Sookie said proudly. "Doesn't she look just like a princess?"

"Yeah," Dean agreed, "she looks beautiful."

"Mom made the dress," I told them.

"Not to mention the girl inside it," Mom added.

"Hello, gross," I said.

"I'm just saying," Mom commented.

"I'm getting kind of nervous," I confessed.

"Oh, you're gonna be great," Lane said.

Behind them, the crowd began to move. "I think act three's starting," I told Lane.

"Henry's act!" Lane said excitedly. "How do I look?"

"You might want to hold a phone in front of your face so he'll recognize you," I said to her. Lane smiled at me. "Bye." She ran off, pushing through the crowd as Paris appeared, grabbing my arm. "I need you!" And she dragged me out into the hall. "He's not here!" she said frantically.

"Who's not here?" I asked.

"Tristin! I've looked everywhere! I called his home! His cell! I called three girls I know he's seeing!"

"Paris, calm down."

She turned to face me. "Weren't you listening? He's not here! We're on in twenty minutes and we don't have a Romeo! We are going to fail!"

"We're not going to fail."

"Do you think Harvard accepts people who fail Shakespeare? They don't! I don't have the numbers on it or anything, but I feel pretty secure in saying, you fail Shakespeare, you don't get into Harvard!"

"Okay, well maybe he's just in one of the bathrooms smoking," I suggested.

"Good idea," Paris said. "You check the east men's rooms! I'll check the west ones!" Paris went off in one direction while I headed the other way. We met up in a hallway on the other side of the building a few minutes later, Tristin-less. Paris was even more worked up than before. "I knew he was going to do this! But no one wanted to listen to me! It was all, 'Let's make Tristin Romeo, he's hot!'"

"What about Brad?" I asked as we walked toward Grand Hall.

"Brad transferred schools," Paris replied.

We rounded a corner and suddenly Tristin was there.

"Where've you been?" Paris demanded to know. "You have to get dressed! We're on in ten minutes!"

"Can't," Tristin answered.

"What?" Paris stared at him.

"Actually, my dad had me pulled out of school. He—"
Tristin started to explain, but Paris didn't wait to hear
the rest. She took off and disappeared around the corner. "And is she unhappy," Tristin finished.

"What do you mean he pulled you out of school?
What happened?" I asked.

"Nothing. Just ticked the old man off that's all."

"By doing what? Tristin? Come on. Tell me."

"I got into some trouble."

"Trouble . . . involving . . ."

"Involving Duncan and Bowman. And . . . Bowman's dad's safe," Tristin reluctantly admitted.

"Oh no."

"I mean, Bowman had a key, it was supposed to be no
big deal, but then that crazy silent alarm kicked in . . ."

"You broke into Bowman's dad's safe," I stated, a
look of disgust on my face.

"Yes."

"Stupid."

"Yes," he repeated quietly.

"Well, okay, you can apologize, right? And put back
the money and you can explain that, I don't know, you
were going through something."

"I was. I was going through his safe."

"Why would you do this?"

"I don't know. I guess that's something I can ponder
at military school."

"Military school?"

"The police are letting our parents handle it, and in
my case, that means military school in North Carolina."

"I don't know what to say."

"I imagine you're overwhelmed by the relief at
knowing that soon I will be gone."

I looked at him a beat. "I am so sorry," I said sincerely.

"I'm a big boy," he said, dropping his attitude. "I can handle it."

"There's nothing you can—"

"No. My dad actually came home from Fiji for this. He doesn't come home from Fiji for anything."

A man appeared at the end of the hall. "Tristin," he called. "Come on."

"I gotta go," Tristin said. He leaned slightly toward me. "So . . . I'd kiss you goodbye, but, uh . . ." He gestured toward the doorway. "Your boyfriend's watching." I looked over and saw Dean eyeing Tristin's every move.

He looked back at me. "Take care of yourself . . ." He paused a moment, then smiled and added, "Mary." I smiled back at the memory. And I watched him head down the hall to his father. It was kinda sad to see him go, especially like this.

Then Paris appeared, dressed as Romeo. "What're you standing there for? Let's go! And you'd better start sucking on an Altoid!" I followed her into Grand Hall to perform our act. Despite all the interference, the act turned out well, and for now, Harvard is safe.

It was an immense relief to have this done and I ran to the coatroom to meet Mom and Sookie. We grabbed Dean and Lane and returned to Stars Hollow. Lane had to get home, but Mom, Sookie, Dean, and I went on to Luke's to celebrate. "Hey, so did you and Paris actually kiss or was that like a stage thing?" Dean asked as we entered the diner.

"A lady never kisses and tells," I told him. We sat at a table as Mom headed to the counter to order us a round of celebratory burgers and chili fries. There wasn't anyone else in the diner, so after a few minutes, Mom convinced Luke to come over and sit with us. Even Jess seemed to forget he hated everyone in the world and brought us some pie before he disappeared upstairs. A few minutes later, "Lovefool" by the Cardigans started playing in the diner. Luke got up to get Jess to shut off the music, but Mom stopped him and told him to have more tea. And then "#1 Crush" by Garbage came on and I realized Jess was playing us songs from Baz Luhrmann's Romeo and Juliet soundtrack. The Butt-hole Surfers were up next with "Whatever (I Had a Dream)," as we gathered our things together to leave, saying our good nights and heading out the door. Luke locked up behind us and I heard Jess put on his final song for the evening, a non-soundtrack tune, and through the open window from Luke's apartment, the Vandals sang "So Long, Farewell" as we walked home.